Davy Chadwick

Davy Chadwick

JAMES BUCHAN

HAMISH HAMILTON

By the same author

A PARISH OF RICH WOMEN

HAMISH HAMILTON LTD

Penguin Books Ltd, 27 Wrights Lane, London W8 5TZ (Publishing & Editorial)
and Harmondsworth, Middlesex, England (Distribution & Warehouse)
Viking Penguin Inc., 40 West 23rd Street, New York, New York 10010, U.S.A.
Penguin Books Australia Ltd, Ringwood, Victoria, Australia
Penguin Books Canada Limited, 2801 John Street, Markham, Ontario, Canada
L3R 1B4
Penguin Books (N.Z.) Ltd, 182–190 Wairau Road, Auckland 10, New Zealand

First published in Great Britain 1987 by
Hamish Hamilton Ltd

Copyright © 1987 by James Buchan

British Library Cataloguing in Publication Data

Buchan, James, *1954–*
Davy Chadwick.
I. Title
823'.914[F]   PR6052.U215
ISBN 0–241–12115–9

Set in 12/13pt Palatino by Butler & Tanner Ltd
Printed and bound in Great Britain by
Butler & Tanner Ltd, Frome and London

for Evelyn

ONE

by John Chadwick

My son, Davy Chadwick, was abducted from my house in southern Italy in the late afternoon of 15 December 1984. He is aged five years and ten months. It is now the evening of 16 December. I have not yet found him. I am trying to find him.

I have thought it necessary to keep a record of my actions. This is not because I fear I might be misunderstood. I do not care for the opinions of people outside my family circle. If Davy comes to hear this record, his safety will have justified the steps I took.

This account is an exercise in recollection. I am searching for clues to Davy's abduction. I have ransacked my memory of the past thirty hours. I must now go back further into the past, to the beginning of my life in Italy.

I moved to Italy to please Dawn, my wife and Davy's mother. I met her first in Kensington, on the evening of 1 June 1978, at the house of a banker acquaintance, William Nelson. In those days, I was a stockbroker. I analysed building stocks for Mowbray de Salle Smith. I lived alone in Clapham. I did not like my colleagues in the City and what little I had in common with my friends from Cambridge such as Nelson was vanishing as each of us became self-absorbed.

Nelson had a horse running somewhere. He had been drinking all day. The room was crowded and thick with cigarette smoke, which I dislike. I did not wish to stay.

I made my way to the door. I saw a girl, standing with her back to the fireplace. She was not smoking or drinking champagne, like the other guests. In her glass was a brown liquid, which I later found to have been beer. She seemed to know nobody. I presumed Nelson had invited her, but he

1

had done well at the races and was ignoring her.

She did not look out of the ordinary. She had blonde hair, blue eyes and a dress to her knees. Yet she did not seem like any girl I had seen before. I stood before her to introduce myself and saw that it was not shyness that kept her standing alone in front of the fireplace. She had nothing to say and nothing she wished to hear. We slept together that night, which surprised me.

We spent our evenings talking in Chelsea restaurants until their proprietors came to know us and we were overcharged. Dawn was thrifty. She travelled only by bus, though she was punctual. When she paid with a cheque, she held the pen like a paintbrush, in her left hand, the wrist turned in an awkward curve above the line.

Both her parents had died, her father that spring, her mother years before on the liner *Lakonia*, which caught fire at sea. Her father was called Geoffrey Durward. He had owned a brickworks in Bedfordshire but shown no interest in it. He had sold the business to London Brick in the 1960s and retired, with what Dawn called his things, to a house near Naples. At his death, she had an income from a small family trust. It paid for the upkeep of the Italian house and allowed her the luxury of studying drawing at the Slade. She had ambitions to paint for a living. She was finishing a picture for the Summer Exhibition at Burlington House. She was otherwise uneducated.

Her foreign upbringing made her unpredictable. Three weeks after our first meeting, the subject of marriage arose. Dawn refused to marry in church. Her father had disapproved of religion. She said she had no close relations. My parents gave us a reception at their house in Bournemouth. It was 21 June 1978. Nelson was my best man but made no speech. Dawn had asked that there be no speech. After an hour, Nelson fell asleep, as he often did in public, and we stepped out of the house, leaving the back door open.

I had chosen Venice for our honeymoon. The pictures we saw made a bond between us and a gulf between me and my old world. We would sit together, over lunch in the Giudecca, attributing this to Sebastiano and that to Giorgione, till the afternoon was gone. In the Gesuiti, she banged her shin against a step while peering at a dirty Titian. Walking became painful to her. We decided to spend our second week at the house in the south.

In Venice, we had been wrapped in crowds. We were alone on the journey south. We travelled by sleeper to Rome and there changed. The country was new to me and Dawn could tell me nothing. The train began to amble. Views of the sea became infrequent. For long periods, we halted among factories with broken windows. Weeds grew between the railway lines. The compartment became hot and we became hungry. Dawn stared out of the window, saying little, anxious not to miss our station. When I questioned her, she snapped at me.

At last we stopped at a place marked Bocca d'Oro. It was mid-afternoon. The empty platform looked like any other we had halted and waited at, and passed. Some oleanders dangled out of a tub. There was a bar. Its interior flashed with zinc. A guard walked down the platform, banging the wheels of the train.

I suggested we take a taxi.

She said, 'Don't worry. You're probably dying for a drink.' She limped into the shade of the booking hall.

I took the suitcases into the bar. In the darkness, I drank a cup of tea, made in a glass by a girl of twelve years old. I peered into the empty booking hall and out to a small square in front of the station, which was planted with pollarded plane trees. It was empty. I asked the girl a question and then repeated it. I sat down.

A young man hurried in and picked up both suitcases. I rose to my feet but he was gone, bustling out through the booking hall and into the square. Dawn was seated in the back of a yellow taxi.

I asked Dawn where she had been.

She said, 'Giuseppe was at his cousin's.'

I suppose Giuseppe was the name of the taxi-driver, but thought it better to save my questions. In any case, we had not gone a hundred yards before he stopped, sprang out and opened her door, and they were gone, rattling on the steel blind of a closed supermarket; and then a pharmacy, an ironmonger's, a stationer's and a dirty house, ochre in colour, for which the young man had a key. Each time they returned, he was carrying brown paper bags which he laid in the boot.

The next time we stopped, Giuseppe jumped out, but this time to open a pair of wrought-iron gates. Beyond was a gravel path, lined with urns of geraniums, and a large house at the end. On each side of the path, stone pines were planted thickly. The sunlight reached the floor in patches.

The house was round, and covered with creeper except for a tower which came out of the foliage in a muddle of plaster moulding. From below I could see moulded railway trains, factories and small aircraft. A woman with flowing drapery led an army of workmen forward. Beneath the tower, a double staircase, with a wrought-iron balustrade, snaked up to a french door. I walked up one side.

Dawn cried up at me, 'Don't. Giuseppe does it.'

I looked to the side. The young man was halfway up the wall, shinning neatly up the creeper till he reached the tower. He vanished through the porthole of a plaster ocean liner. Dawn had her arms round her chest, as if cold.

I said, 'What a delightful monstrosity, Dawn.'

She did not hear me, or did not want to answer. The young man came out of a little door under the balustrade and hurried to the car boot. I went to help him, but he was once again too quick. He disappeared inside the house with a torch and a screwdriver. I followed him in.

The passage was narrow, dark and cool. It smelt of England: a mixture of paraffin, cigar ash and alcohol. As I walked carefully down, Giuseppe's torch came on. He had found a fuse-box. There were different smells: bad electrical connections, gas, fruit and simple cooking.

A light came on, scarcely brighter than the torch. It showed a curved passage with a sea-green carpet and walls covered in pictures and china, Giuseppe started to wind a clock. It sent chimes along the passage ahead of us.

I followed him up a staircase, stopping as he pulled dust sheets off chairs and clocks. We came to a long, curving gallery. The floor was of large green tiles and the dust sheets showed it was sparsely furnished. Giuseppe was now throwing back shutters. For the difference he made to the light in the room, they might just as well have stayed closed.

As he pulled back the shutters from the french doors in the middle, I saw that Dawn was standing on the balcony outside, her arms still clasped under her breast. Above her head, I could see the sea beyond Bocca d'Oro.

'Welcome,' said Giuseppe in English.

As he helped her over the threshold, she smiled at me and said, 'Giuseppe will get you something to drink from the cellar.'

TWO

by John Chadwick

It was at that moment, as the young man helped Dawn over the threshold of the Villa Crespi, that I first questioned whether I would return to London.

I had no attachment to Clapham, in the midst of a timid rejuvenation, or to stockbroking. Much of my time was wasted. Hard work, then fashionable in the City under the influence of New York, was a distraction. Most stock-market analysis was less useful than spinning a coin. I had no particular desire to spend my life enriching my private clients or the future beneficiaries of pension funds. As for my friends, I scarcely saw them. They were busy reproducing themselves or amassing capital gains from moving house every year.

I knew that if I stayed in London, I would end up with a partnership and a good income, which had eluded my father. Unlike my father, who started in the City as a clerk, I wondered if this were much of a life. I knew that I could invest more successfully away from the gossip and claptrap of Mowbrays.

I tried to explain these things to Dawn the first evening at the villa. She was drying sheets before a gas-bottle fire. She nodded. It had not occurred to her that I might wish to live elsewhere than in Italy. Or at the Villa Crespi.

It was only later that I realised the house had moulded Dawn's nature. It was chaotic. The objects in the public rooms, which ran in a curved enfilade the circumference of the house, were arranged without reference to period. Precious clocks from England stood beside Venetian blackamoors or Futurist steel sculpture. Dawn, too, had no notion of the past as a hierarchy of events receding out of view, but as a sort of closed space to cross, as she crossed these jumbled rooms, holding a duster. The books were as disorderly as her reading, English with Italian, history with verse, and gaping with holes. Neither the shelves nor Dawn had any political economy, geography or philosophy.

The house was an absurd place, but it had been adequately managed. There was no farmland. The garden trees needed no tending. The clocks functioned as soon as they were wound. The electrical connections were no worse than those in our Venice hotel, the pictures no dirtier than in the Frari. No burglar had a chance against the window bars, which seemed such bagatelles from outside and were so massive from within. The roof looked sound.

The villa might have been abandoned before an approaching army. The kitchen was stocked with dried or tinned food. Giuseppe took me down to the cellar. It was lined from floor to rafters with racks of wine, white from Ischia and red from the slopes of Vesuvius. There were 1,170 bottles divided equally between each vintage from 1967 to 1977. Dawn asked me to taste the early vintage at once, for they were deteriorating. Opened, they smelled of honey and roses and were vinegar in an hour. Half the cellar floor was taken by demijohns of oil. I did not need to audit these. They would last us our actuarial lifetimes.

In Bocca d'Oro, too, it was as if Dawn had not been away. The day after our arrival from Venice, we walked down the hill to the village, arm in arm. She introduced me to the newsagent and a police officer, the laundry woman and the owners of the wine shop and the restaurant. She treated them each with courtesy. She made no adjustment, whether she were talking to an old marquis, whose family had built the villa as a refuge from Naples and who now lived above his paper shop, or to the sexton who would have been locked up in England as insane.

She seemed to have but one way of doing things. I hired the grave-digger's sister to clean the house. I had my hair cut by a deaf-mute barber. I drank a *ramazotti* on credit in the best of the three bars. I began Italian lessons with the priest's nephew. He was an unctuous young man with an affected voice and Dawn disliked him intensely; but it was as if for her there were no other teacher—or barber, or bar or cleaner—in Bocca d'Oro.

When I said we must return, Dawn took no notice. I telephoned the senior partner of Mowbrays and took an extra month's leave. In the course of the month, the lira was devalued. I bought some Antinori champagne to celebrate and quizzed Dawn about the house expenses. In September, I resigned from Mowbrays and put my own house on the market.

I am not extravagant. Dawn never carried money, and she never wanted it from me. Her only luxury was the Italian illustrated newspapers, which she bought for herself each week till her mind was filled with quintuplets and murders. We kept no car. Giuseppe drove us on credit, and charged his own depreciation.

The Clapham house was sold for a good price. I thought that we could live frugally on the income from the re-invested proceeds, and on Dawn's allowance.

I was misinformed. The winter rain plunged through the roof and made a lake of the first-floor saloons. Giuseppe made shift with new tiles but he was as feckless as any Italian. I realised that we should need two million lire a month just to pay our bills and keep the house from falling down.

Davy was born, a month premature, on 12 February 1979, in an infirmary run by Carmelite sisters just up the coast from Bocca d'Oro. Dawn took his birth without complaint. I fretted beside a bar in the infirmary basement, drinking whisky served by a nun from Thirsk. Mother and child stayed in the hospital only two days. The grave-digger's sister had been making clothes. Other children's paraphernalia could be had at knock-down prices from among the postcards and artists' materials in Crespi's shop. But the bill, when it arrived from the infirmary, troubled me.

Davy was a sickly baby. Dawn was unable to keep him quiet. I was haunted by the expense of his falling ill.

Dawn was always naïve in matters of money. I mentioned the problem to her one evening, as we sat by Davy's cot in the tower room she had set up as a nursery. She merely looked up and smiled and said, 'What's wrong with Bots?'

I was learning Italian from the financial newspaper, *Il Sole-24 Ore*. I knew already that these were a Treasury Bill, issued in profusion by a spendthrift State, and carrying a very high yield, I think about 16 percent in those days.

I explained to her carefully that we would need more than 150 million lire even of such high-yielding tax-free instruments to maintain our standard of living, and we would still be at the mercy of inflation. Our capital base was too narrow. We must either broaden our capital base or I must invest more aggressively than in Italian Government bonds.

She became flustered, and began to feed the child, which she did too often out of nerves. She begged me not to invest in the stock market, which had done her father no good. The capital was hers as much as mine.

Then she said, 'We could sell something. My father used to.'

I protested. I told her it was irresponsible and selfish to think of liquidating Davy's physical patrimony while he fed at her breast. I said it was futile to sell the house, which was our reason for being in Italy. She broke in with a catalogue of objects from Doccia plates to the Guido Reni that were saleable and scattered about the house. She said there was an inventory, which an old auctioneer from Zürich called Jakob Hoffmann had made after her father's death. She would find it for me, if only Davy would stop crying. Then she became sentimental about the old man. She spoke of a large hotel where they had stayed in Zürich, and chocolate wrapped in bread at Spruengli. Soon both mother and child were crying.

There were two inventories. One was in Italian, typed carefully and sealed by a notary. It showed values in lire that looked pessimistic even to an inexperienced eye. I could not follow the legal Italian. I suspected the list was a probate valuation. The second was in pencil and written in bad English. In this, the old Jew showed no interest in the subject or attribution of a work of art. It took me half the morning

9

to connect *'Big naked woman goldframed'* with the Guido. The pencilled values were also lire and not much higher than the official values for probate; or so I thought, until I reached the last page and saw that they were 1978 Swiss francs. I went down to play with Davy for an hour. I saw we had no choice.

We left Davy with the cleaning woman and took four candlesticks—marked *'Very nice lights'* in the inventory—in a false suitcase with us on the train. I did not know Zürich. Dawn insisted on a ludicrously expensive hotel called the Baur au Lac. The next morning, we were to breakfast at Spruengli. Our path was blocked by a large man in a fawn cashmere overcoat and a bright blue silk hat. Beneath the hat, long white hair spread in all directions. He had thick white sideburns. I took Dawn's arm. She burst into tears.

The man opened his arms wide and said, 'You have not changed at all. I knew I could still ambush you in Paradeplatz.'

She leaned on his chest so long that ladies stared from the tram stop. She extricated herself and said, 'Herr Hoffmann, this is my husband, John Chadwick.'

He examined me for a moment, screwing up small eyes. Then he took my right arm in both hands and said, as if to himself, 'Aha, a husband. And a father, too, who does not delay.' He laughed abruptly.

I ignored his coarseness. The eccentricity of the meeting place in Paradeplatz, with the Swiss ladies eyeing us from the tram stop, dressed-up and patient as a wedding queue, made his manner more absurd than repulsive. He was big, loud and unexpected. He held my arm till I withdrew it. I noticed that he had fine hands, with long delicate fingers. They added to his ugliness. They might have been stolen from a woman and attached to his great paws. In Spruengli, where he joined us for breakfast, he kept touching Dawn's hair and face with these fingers, which excited interest from the Swiss.

His saleroom was off the Bahnhofstrasse. Inside, vintage cars had been hoisted one above the other on cranes.

He took me aside, and hissed in my ear, 'Do you wish to see the pornographic watches?'

I said, 'Don't you think we should do our business first?'

'Of course,' he said and ushered us into an untidy office. Seated at a desk was a young man in a skullcap. 'I started with watches, you know. I only keep them on to annoy the good doctor. Frau Dr Schoppe!' He bellowed for this lady.

A bun of white hair peered round the door. I offered her my seat, but she demurred and stood with her back to the wall.

Hoffmann was holding Dawn's hand across the desk. He asked, 'So what treasures have you brought me, apart from yourself?'

I drew the candlesticks out of their newspaper and placed them on his desk. 'We thought they might be Amsterdam.'

'Naturally. I remember them. First-quality work. 50,000 francs reserve for each pair.'

Dr Schoppe became agitated. 'Might I just interject here, Herr Hoffmann, but I believe the young man is correct. Amsterdam, about 1610, I would venture. Unfortunately, I cannot read the maker's mark.'

'Of course you can't! Go and get the Cornelius, First Volume.'

She scampered from the room.

Hoffmann poured himself a glass of water from a red Bohemian glass jug, drank it off and refilled it. 'What a stupid woman. Ariel is stupid too, aren't you, my boy? But he knows what to do. He can scarcely read. But he knows how to find me Dr Cornelius himself in Den Haag and Schmidt in Hamburg. Won't you, Arik?'

There followed two conversations on the telephone, Hoffmann spoke a mishmash of languages, all incorrectly. He began softly. Yes, they were in some doubt about the master. The mark was a bell, yes. Of course, he should have known from the quality and, yes, Frau Dr Schoppe was looking in the great work. But then they had none of the learning of a Dr Cornelius or a Professor Schmidt. And the estimate. Really, only 30,000 francs, for the quality? Still, they would go into the next sale. Yes, on the 27th. In person? What a pleasure that would be! Business in Zürich, really! On the way to Ascona, indeed!

11

'As I thought, 50,000 francs each pair. Foolish woman. Those two will be down here, sniffing like dogs. They'll bid each other up and end up with a pair each. Nazis, of course, both of them. Brown as shit.' He drank another glass of water and beamed at us. 'Ariel will write you a cheque for 100,000 francs.'

I was having none of that. I said, 'Wouldn't it be better to wait for the sale?'

Dawn looked at me pleadingly. 'Shut up, John. You are so kind, Herr Hoffmann.'

'Aha, he does not trust me. That's a good husband.'

I hesitated and then, solely to please her, accepted the cheque from the young man. That she trusted him was recommendation enough, though I found something strange about their affection. In the street, he put his arm through hers and she did not flinch. At dinner that evening in his house, he served her first and waited until she had tasted the meat. The son seemed to admire Dawn no less. He stared at her from across the table. He did not speak unless spoken to.

Hoffmann told me his history without prompting. His father had been a great Talmudic scholar in Prague before the war. He had had all his children learn a trade: cobbling, carpet-weaving and watch-repair for Jakob, who was the youngest and quickest. Eichmann, who interviewed the rabbi himself in execrable Hebrew, sent them to Theresienstadt. The children plied their trades and were told it was a good camp. Trains took all but the youngest to extinction. Starving in Soviet Vienna, the boy accosted Dawn's father, a major on the Control Commission. His filthy waistcoat was hung with repeaters. He made the crossing to the Allied sectors under the seat of an American jeep.

While he told this story, he held Dawn's hand. He was evidently grateful to her father, who had helped set him up in Zürich. He had accompanied father and daughter on jaunts across middle Europe and stuffed her with chocolate and presents in Zürich. It was then that Dawn learned the smattering of European languages that was the nearest thing she had to an education.

Hoffmann, who seemed illiterate in every language, kept dropping out of English, but Dawn followed, like a beagle pursuing a hare.

With each language she spoke, her nature underwent an adjustment. In French, she was garrulous and vapid; in German, deductive or sweeping; in Italian, refined. When Hoffmann bowed to say his prayers, Dawn murmured responses. I saw that the Dawn I had married was just a facet of a multiple nature: the vague, scatter-brained English side of her. Whole tracts of her life, including her curious friendship with Hoffmann, were closed to me.

Hoffmann took command. He took us to the Creditanstalt, where a small man invested our new capital in stocks and bonds in a minute. When I said we would declare the account to the Italian tax authorities, the man fell silent and stared at his desk. I might have uttered an obscenity. At length, he said that the Major Durward had used a coded account and a private telephone number. I gave in. When we left, his desk was as empty as when we entered. We dined with him at his home that night. His conversation was dull beyond description, and his wife timid. I despaired of the account. It was only at our next meeting, where he produced a return of 25 percent, that I saw his dullness was affectation. His mind was sharp and corrupt.

I saw Hoffmann's pornographic watches. They were as I expected. He showed the anatomical curiosity of a child, while Dr Schoppe hissed dates and provenances over my shoulder, her face hidden in embarrassment. His breath was stale and he drank water incessantly. But his predictions were accurate. The candlesticks sold for exactly 50,000 francs a pair, one to Schmidt, one to Cornelius. The 'Good Dutch skating', which we rolled up and took that autumn, was attributed by Dr Schoppe to Hobbema. It sold for 300,000 francs, as Hoffmann had said it would.

Relieved, I called a halt to these jaunts. We now had the income to live as I had always wanted to live. We did not seek company and did not reject it. Visitors came from

England, on their way to Capri or Amalfi. I enjoyed their visits but our friends seemed unable to stay in one place. They jumped into hired cars to visit Pompeii or Paestum, as if these places had anything to offer them in half an afternoon. They stayed up late and rose early and left, I suspect, with relief.

They called us *rentiers* and yet speculated themselves in new stock-market issues and London property. They said I must be bored without a job. I said I had a job: a wife, and a child, and a library approaching 20,000 volumes which I was building in the circular room that formed the centre of the first-floor *piano nobile*. They said Dawn must be lonely without friends. I said she had friends: the young *marchesa* Crespi and Amina, the servant, and a whole village of women. They said I was getting out of touch. I said I read the Italian newspapers and the *Financial Times*, or at least the back halves of them. They invited us to their weddings. We did not go. There was so much to do.

I was happy watching Davy grow. He had his mother's blonde hair and blue eyes, but what was commonplace in England was an Italian prodigy. To watch him teasing Amina as she pounded after him, or talking Italian to himself or playing on his own, so self-possessed and free of care, pleased me each day. His toys strewed the house. Our mealtimes altered. On the edge of the cliff, Dawn built a wall to protect him. Giuseppe looked on dubiously, but she had learned something in her father's brickfields.

I did not miss my family. My mother came once. She had no experience away from home. Naples alarmed her and she did not like the heat. She quarrelled with Dawn's regime for Davy and complained about dirt. She was not able to look after herself and Dawn and Amina did nothing to help her.

Dawn used to talk about William Nelson. She was ever inviting him to stay and he on the point of coming, on the way back from Egypt or Yemen or wherever. He is one of those men who cannot keep to a plan. He would telephone at last from London, during dinner or after we were in bed, saying that he could not come after all.

He came in the end, on 13 December, for Christmas. Two days later, Davy was taken.

THREE

by William Nelson

It is a cold, damp, cluttered house. I scarcely recognise it or the people in it. I hesitated at the back door, while a young man carried my suitcase before me, calling for me to be careful. He had accosted me at the station and run away with my things to a yellow taxi. For all I knew, he might have picked up the wrong guest, and I would be expelled from the passage into a room full of strangers.

I know that my last visit was in April, 1978. I think the house was dark and cool, perhaps because umbrella pines grow thickly in front of the windows. I remember Dawn was there, and her father. I read the old man stock-market reports from week-old newspapers after lunch and memoirs after dinner. I suppose I went for walks with Dawn on the cliffs and to the village. We might have bathed.

I do not remember much more; not the house, which is round like some latter-day Castel Sant'Angelo, nor the creeper all over it, nor the tower covered in fascist stucco-work; not even the railway station and the square with lopped plane trees.

Today is 14 December and it is cold. The walls run with damp and the passages, even at midday, are black as night. Someone has put time-switches on the electric passage-lights. The light keeps flicking off and I have to feel my way along the dripping wall, dislodging a plate or a picture to smash on the flags.

Not that anyone seems to notice. For two days, I have hardly seen my hosts or the little boy. I breakfast alone, and Chadwick was absent both nights at dinner. Most doors are locked and some doors open one day are locked the next. As I wander, the servant woman sometimes labours past me and giggles when we touch for she is very fat. Opening a door, I hear the pant and the pounding tail of a dog. Once, when I was reading in the big circular library, Chadwick passed diagonally before me, dressed in a mackintosh and holding the newspapers. I see him in the passage downstairs, looking closely at a piece of paper under the light. I approach, but the light goes and I must stop and steady myself against a wall. I listen for them, and think I hear something, but then Dawn shouts my name from two feet away; or a clock chimes out the hour, the half or the quarter, ringing through the damp gloom like the peel of a flooded belfry.

Even in the light, no two of the clocks show the same time. Yet the life of Villa Crespi is constructed on a notion of correct time: that lunch is punctual at one and dinner at nine, that the train for Naples sometimes leaves early and the newspapers always arrive late. For all I know, Chadwick keeps somewhere a master clock whose time corresponds to the station clock in Bocca d'Oro or the newsagent's watch. I have not found it. The house gets up when Davy needs attention and goes to bed when Chadwick pads in to say he has set the burglar alarm. There does not seem to be an alternative.

'Lazy,' said Davy. 'Get up, lazy, lazy,' he said when I tried to lie in on the first morning. I turned over, tired from my train journey, but he dropped a toy on my bed, jumped onto the window sill and tugged at the curtains till two rings came away. That night I tried to stay up reading in the library, but Chadwick gave me such long instructions about locks and burglar alarms, and then kept opening the door and listening, that I closed the book and went to bed.

The waking interval between sleep cannot be longer than twelve hours; but in this period, all is confusion. The smallest activity requires hours of preparation, a journey days. The taxi-driver had not put my suitcase down in the hall upstairs before Chadwick was telling him when to pick me up again.

Food is delivered each day at noon. This is announced the night before, mentioned at any opportunity during the morning and greeted with a barrage of shouts down the passages. A visit to the shops themselves begins with a burst of shouting; for the keys or the letters to go, or the dog's lead, or Davy's walking-shoes. I hear marshalling in the dark passage that leads to the back door; a search for money; last insructions from Dawn. Then the procession sets off, the dog pulling, Davy leading or lagging, and still the shouting winding down the shallow hill to Bocca d'Oro till it is lost in the lee of the pines.

Was Dawn always like this? Was Chadwick? I can't really remember. Dawn was always a bit odd. I liked her because she was different from anybody else I knew. Chadwick was shy at Cambridge, and frugal. I can't believe their life together was always so chaotic or rather, not chaotic but circumscribed by a lunatic order. In a while, I, too, shall have perfect night sight, sleep too long and shout when I need something.

That's why I am writing this. I went down to Bocca d'Oro this morning and bought an exercise book off the most learned stationer I have ever met. He spoke beautiful English with a slight drawl and made me coffee on a gas-ring at his feet. When I told him I was starting a diary, he clapped his hands together.

I have found a place, under an old almond tree behind the kitchen, where I can sit after lunch with a pot of coffee and my exercise book, safe from being called to do some job for Dawn. Above me, I can hear Chadwick talking to himself behind barred windows. Above him, Dawn is singing in the tower. Davy himself is playing just around the curved wall of the house.

It is a curious game. It is as if Davy is becoming as set in eccentric ways as his parents. I see only that part of it where he races into view of my position under the tree, spreads his arms wide and falls, a little gingerly, to the ground. He then passes slowly back out of sight behind the house where the hidden part of the game probably repeats itself for he is soon racing back into view. I can hear what he is saying quite clearly: 'Sono Davy, sono Davy,' over and over again.

'Willie!'

I can hear Dawn in the passage, throwing open doors. It is time for Davy's walk. Whether it is three o'clock or four

18

o'clock, it is still time for Davy's walk, though yesterday Davy had no walk at all.

I walked round the side of the house and saw her putting Davy into his coat. I envied her manner, which was both rough and gentle.

'Willie, will you take Davy with you on your walk?'

'Am I going for a walk?'

'You always used to at this time, didn't you?'

'Oh did I? Come on, Dave, let's go.'

Davy looked at me suspiciously from within his undone coat. 'I want my drum.'

I had brought him the drum from Eyup. I was flattered.

'No, Davy,' said Dawn. 'Because mama is painting it. When she's finished,' she said and then to me, 'You won't let him near the cliff, will you, you promise?'

'Drum.'

'No, Davy, I said no. Willie, perhaps it's better not.'

'Now, don't worry.' I put my arm round her shoulders. 'Don't be such a fusspot. We won't go anywhere near the cliff.'

Mother and child looked at me dubiously. 'I suppose you could take the dog and just go to the lighthouse.'

'No dog. Let's go, Dave.'

Our path lay through the gates and down the road to Bocca d'Oro, before branching off through a row of modern villas with painted gates and gardens of conifers and rosemary. Dawn cried something after us, but we pressed on. On our right, the village and the sea were in full view; on our left, the cliff on which Villa Crespi stood at first blocked out the sea. The land forms a sort of promontory that runs on down about a mile to what looks like a defunct lighthouse and a concrete platform for bathing.

'Do you like your school, Davy?' Even with children, I feel I have to talk; and Davy had spoken not at all as he hurried along beside me, too old to waddle, but not quite upright in his big coat. I wished I were the sort of person who could dramatise the world for children, conjuring brigands behind bushes and treasure in storm grates.

19

'No. Mi non piaciono le suore.'

'Davy, you must speak in English when you speak to me. And you mustn't say such things about the sisters.'

The boy looked at me carefully and then skipped on ahead. I had made a mistake; perhaps Italian was his language, and English for use only with grown-ups, among whom I had now placed myself. I preferred to be Italian to him, like Amina and the young man who drove the taxi and did work around the house. I wished I had insisted on the drum.

'Do you want to see my place?' Davy had stopped and was shifting from foot to foot at a point where a lane ran off between the villas to the left.

'Yes please, Davy.' I was glad to be in his good books again.

The lane was tarmaced at first, and then narrowed to a muddy track which soon became indistinguishable from the edges of the terraces; but Davy seemed to know where he was going. As we climbed, the signs of cultivation disappeared. The terraces were broken down. We passed a hut without a door and came on open ground covered with heather. The wind was cold and damp. I feared rain. Davy had begun to puff.

'Do you want a ride?' I asked, though I was panting myself.

'No thank you'. Davy just pressed on and upwards, his quilted coat spreading out behind him in the wind. I thought then that he was a determined child, bent almost double over his small steps, and wished he had been mine; or that a child of mine, a girl perhaps, were holding on to my hand as Davy led us up the hill.

'Pooh!'

'What sort of smell? I can never smell anything.'

'Nice, like Mina.' He ran off the path and picked a handful of something from the heather. It was French lavender, though not yet in flower. I recognised the strong, sharp smell.

The zig-zag path was now taking us back in the direction of the house. The top of the ridge still rose two hundred or so feet above us but, a short distance ahead, it dipped and I saw the sea on that side for the first time.

We began to descend, Davy adopting a strange tiptoe as if he were afraid of slipping; but he released my hand when I offered it.

'Sshhh,' he said. 'There are men.'

I found myself tiptoeing. As we came round the head of the cliff, a copse of closely planted trees lurched into view below us. It was surrounded by a high wall, and the sight of this garden, so high up and with the sea on both sides, startled me with pleasure. I wanted to congratulate Davy on his place, but he turned with his finger tight against his lips and nose. He tiptoed quickly down the path, towards a rusty steel gate in the wall. He squeezed through and disappeared.

I could not. The bars of the gate had bent wide enough for a child but not a man, even one as small as I am. The wall was too high to vault and, on the top, broken glass was embedded in a layer of cement. When I threw my coat over the top, I tore the lining. Around the wall, the path was trodden and scattered with litter. One section of wall showed the remains of a stencilled advertisement for beer; but the only other gate was on the cliff side, of all places, where the path petered out into screes and the sight of the sea breaking on rocks below made my head swing.

'Davy!' Once again, I felt foolish in being left behind by a child; but when I peered again through the rusty gate, I could not see him. The pines were planted so closely that little light came down to the rye-grass below. 'Davy!' I shouted again. There was no movement within.

I felt irritated not so much at my exclusion from the garden, but at my irritation; and even the sun, which at that moment broke beneath the cloud layer and bathed the squalid path in gold, could not retrieve my pleasure. I could see the place's charm for Davy: it was secret and remote, and the rye-grass grew unevenly as if over buried walls or paths. Then I remembered Dawn's warning about the cliff and I panicked.

'Davy! Will you come here!'

'Noisy,' said Davy. Even his reappearance took me by surprise.

'Home, old fellow. What a nice place you have.'

'You can come again if she lets you.'

'Thank you. But I have been here before, silly.'

'No, you haven't,' he said and set off on tiptoe back down towards the terraces.

The room where dinner is served is the richest in Villa Crespi and the coldest. The walls are hung in green cut-velvet and ranged along them are life-sized electric candelabra in the form of athletes. The table is a slab of local marble but it might splinter for the weight of silver on it: a vast, crenellated wine cooler, wine pourers, wine coasters, cruet sets in the shape of trains or horse carriages, fork rests, butter dishes, spoon racks.

The abundance of objects reminds me of Chadwick's house in Bournemouth. But evidently Dawn does not share his mother's pride. The silver is polished, but the table is spotted with wax and grease. I saw silver-fish in the water decanters and my glasses were opaque with fingermarks. On the walls there are dark patches where pictures have been removed or replaced with ones smaller and, in the corner, the hanging has come away with the damp. The athletes give next to no light and the gas fire no heat at all, only a dizzying smell of butane. To enter the room is to slide into a cold, dark, stagnant pool.

The dinner that evening was not elegant. It may have been the cold but Chadwick was never seated for longer than a minute at a time, padding down to the cellar for wine or a cylinder for the fire or serving the food, for the servant woman had gone home. I gave up counting the courses: a piece of fatty sausage marooned on a fine plate was followed by claggy Milanese rice, a tiny piece of eel, a veal cutlet full of string, then mashed potato, bread-and-butter pudding, tangerines, half a ricotta. Chadwick himself cleared his plate in two mouthfuls before padding off again.

In his absences, Dawn stared into the electric candles around the walls. She seemed to feel no social compunction to talk. Only when I lit a cigarette after the meal did she get up to find me an ashtray—a Derby saucer—before returning to her dreaming. She plied me with wine, forgetting that I do not drink.

'Davy showed me his place,' I said for want of anything more interesting.

'Oh yes.'

'A garden of pines right up on the cliff.'

'Oh Willie, you were careful, weren't you?'

'Of course I was. I'm not that forgetful.'

'We don't go there very much. It's too far for John's walk.'

'Not too far for Davy.'

'No, I suppose not. Soon he'll be able to go there on his own. My father never let me go. He put a wall round it to protect the trees from the goats.'

'Oh, is it yours?' The thought had not occurred to me.

'Yes, well, you see, Tiberius made it.'

'Tacitus, *Annales*, or Suetonius.' Chadwick had returned and was struggling with a corkscrew.

'I must look at that in the morning. Have you got it?'

'Of course I have. PB Lat 211. I understand you once read some Latin.'

The wine was making Chadwick quarrelsome. I did not want to quarrel. 'I've forgotten everything I learned at Cambridge, old boy. I might never have been there.'

'Forgotten everything, you say. That must have taken a long time. I learned how money behaves and I have forgotten nothing.' He laughed in a demonstrative way and then, as his mood changed, with pleasure. 'What you see here, my dear William'—at which point he got up from the table and started pacing—'is a self-contained, functioning organism dependent only marginally on the goodwill of the world and the vigour of international capital markets.' He laughed again but this time a little surlily. 'We have enough provisions in the house to see us through a prolonged bear market when you would be begging your bank to keep you on as tea-boy.'

'John, do be a bit nicer,' Dawn said quietly. 'Willie has a

very good job.'

'So I have heard. But I wonder, William, what you gain from wandering the world, being kidnapped and hijacked and paying out your depositors' money to terrorists. Dawn tells me that is what you are paid to do.'

I glanced at Dawn, but she was looking out into the darkness. 'Somebody has to do it, old boy,' I said.

'Not at all. I'm sure all these Persians and Turks can do without your loans. Your shareholders certainly can, because they'll never be repaid. Why don't you stay at home? But you have no home, Dawn says. No wife, no child, no place except that tip in Kensington. That's why you wander round the world, making a nuisance of yourself.'

'Does Christmas at Villa Crespi fall into the nuisance category?'

'For God's sake, both of you. Do be nicer.'

'We are being nice,' said Chadwick. 'Though how William managed to forget both the sausages and the marmalade—not the most expensive items in London—is quite beyond me. However, William, you are relatively welcome here. You do not cost much. To be accurate, you cost some 15,000 lire a day, excluding any supplementary depreciation on the assets.'

'I won't break anything, if that's what you mean.' I was not prepared to admit the mishaps in the passages.

'Against that, you are of some marginal utility in walking the dog or Davy and providing company for Dawn.'

'If you'll put a value on that, I'll pay the difference.'

But Chadwick's tiresome whimsy had run its course. He stared at me, squinting. 'The Naples train leaves at or around a quarter past eight. I'll tell Giuseppe.'

I was fed up. I rose, but did not answer because Davy was standing in the door. His thumb was in his mouth and there was sleep in his eyes, but he looked as self-assured in his pyjamas as in his coat on the hill. He had the drum round his neck, but no drumsticks.

'Will you go to bed, Davy!' Chadwick shouted so fiercely, I thought the very force of it would propel Davy out of the

24

room and back upstairs.

Davy walked down to his mother and put his head in her lap. 'Go to bed yourself, noisy.'

'Let's all go to bed,' Dawn said. 'Willie must still be exhausted. And Braggiotti's coming to lunch. That's why we're all so over-excited.'

'Who's he?'

'John's *agente*; you know, a bit like a stockbroker. He's coming down from Milan, all the way, specially. John gets so excited and then everybody gets drunk and nobody does any business.'

'Me? Drunk? What a ludicrous suggestion!' Chadwick's mood had changed again, for the better.

'Everybody to bed. It's half past nine. And Oriana is coming too. Willie will like that.'

As I followed her and Davy out into the dim passage, I put a question to her back: 'Do you know if I ever went to that place, the garden at the top? I mean, when I was here before. I can't for the life of me remember. There must be marvellous specimens. Davy found some French lavender.'

'It's a weed really. The goats don't eat it. We must look in Polunin's *Wild Flowers*.'

'But did we go there?'

'Davy's place? I don't know. Perhaps.'

'He didn't. Don't say he did,' cried Davy from the folds of her dress.

'Don't worry about John, Willie. He's just shy after so long.'

The light flicked off and I banged into a table.

FOUR

by William Nelson

I have written nothing for two days. A catastrophe has occurred which has made writing necessary but impossible. This is what happened.

On 15 December, I woke early. My eyes opened on a blond and red blur which was Davy in a scarlet mackintosh. I reached out to touch him but my bed felt wet.

'Davy! What have you done?'

Davy was not to blame. Gusts of rain were spraying the bed from the open window, and water dripped from overhead.

'Davy! What's happening?'

'Dawn's painting my drum in the tower and daddy's upstairs and Mina's helping him and you must help him.' He took a breath and began again. 'Dawn's painting and Giuseppe has his best clothes on. He said so. We're not drowning. He said so.'

'Of course we're not.'

'Willie!' It was Chadwick shouting.

I got up and dressed. On the stairs, an agglomeration of buckets was swaying up towards me. They were perched on the servant woman's head. I relieved her of her burden.

'Breakfast, sir?' She pointed at her mouth like an Arab.

'May I have it in the tower with the signora?'

I followed the stairs up the tower and stopped on the last landing where a door stood open to the attic. Chadwick was standing, his head on one side, marooned in buckets and bowls. They rang with drips in different registers. He appeared to have given up.

I now felt shy of him. 'Your organism doesn't seem so self-contained this morning. I had a bath in bed.'

He was so distracted that it was some time before he looked up at me. 'Well, it has to be defended every now and then. Only the infernal Giuseppe says he can't come up because he's got a suit on. I wonder, William, if I could delegate this sector to you. I have to go and bribe somebody.'

'Of course. Who are you going to bribe?'

He did not answer. 'We generally have a drink in about half an hour.'

'If you want.'

I put Amina's buckets under the more offensive drips and emptied others into a stone sink. Then I went down the last flight of stairs, knocked and entered.

The room was dark and damp. It was a while before I could distinguish Dawn, with her back to me, in a spotless white smock, standing in front of an easel. She held a brush in her left hand, pointed at the floor, and was talking quietly to herself. As I became accustomed to the light, I saw how strange the room was. The walls were circular and pierced with windows of every shape and size: portholes, triangles, f-holes as in a violin, uneven squares. All were blind with rain. In the corner, a child's bed lay athwart the wall while, in the centre of the room, Davy's toys had been scattered across a ratty Caucasian rug. I saw the drum, and a golliwog missing a leg, bricks and books and a train set, a rocking-horse and an old-fashioned biscuit tin. The place felt submerged and calm, as if a liner had come to rest on the sea bottom.

'Can I sit in here, Dawn, while you work?'

'Just,' she said, turning round and crinkling her nose. 'Have a drink. There's some beer in Davy's fridge.'

'Amina's bringing my breakfast up here, if that's all right.'

'Just,' she said, smiling. 'I'm going to fag you to get me a beer.'

As I brought the can to her, she covered the canvas with her smock.

'How can you work in here, in this light? You'll go blind.'

'It's perfect, Willie. Everybody laughs at me, because I only paint things in the house and never people. But this is what I see and live with all winter. I was up here with Davy and saw his toys all scattered on the carpet and I thought, that's what I want, this moment now, I mean Davy now, but his things.' She became flustered and, as if to make up for her speech, said: 'Do you want to see what I've done? You won't make arty-farty comments, will you?'

I walked over to her and put my hand on her shoulder. She had begun with the rocking-horse and the drum; the biscuit tin, the toys and the pattern on the carpet were barely sketched. A wet light leaked onto this muddle and transformed it into an arrangement as orderly as a landscape with figures or a bunch of snowdrops in a jar. Perhaps it was the dreary light in the picture, which teemed in layers between the eye and the picture plane, which gave me a sense of intrusion and expectancy; as if something were about to occur or had happened but was not yet discovered.

This seemed a literary judgment and I feared annoying her. I cast round for something else to say.

'Who's that on the tin?'

'Oh, that's my grandmother. She was very pretty and won a competition from the biscuit company and then married my grandfather, who was only a farmer then.'

'I thought he made bricks.'

'He did. But that was only after they had found clay in his fields.' She looked at me with such enthusiasm that I laughed. 'They built a kiln, I suppose it was in the 1920s sometime, but the bricks were so good, such a beautiful red all-through colour and so strong, that he went into partnership with a solicitor in Sandy and gave up farming altogether.'

I stopped laughing. 'Did you know him?'

'I don't really know. He died in 1960, aged eighty, so I could have done, but I'm not sure. You never know with adults, because they tell you things and then say you remember them but I think I do remember one thing. A tall, old man being led round the works by my father. My grandfather was certainly blind at the end. I think I remember him stopping, just before the tunnel kiln where the bricks were fired, and saying to my father, "Stop." Just like that. Then he went over to the pallet, where the green bricks were stacked ready for going through the kiln, and pulled them out, one after the other, feeling them with his fingers and then dropping them to the ground. I'm sure I remember the green bricks all broken on the ground. Amina, thank you so much.'

I took the tray from the servant, dropped it and caught it again as Davy rolled out from under her apron, shrieking with laughter and still wearing his bright red mackintosh, Amina was cackling so much I thought she would fall, too.

'Now, Dave, come and sit with me on the bed. I'll do you some toast and marmalade. Thank you, Amina.'

He cast an interested eye at his toys, but joined me quietly on the bed, gazing at us in turn.

'What happened to your magnificent brickworks?'

'Oh, don't talk about it. My father sold it because he lost interest, or rather, after he'd married and they'd moved to Newmarket, he thought it was a bit grubby or something. He was a crashing snob.'

'Well, bricks are grubby.'

'Typical of you to say that. Nothing has changed. In that sort of world, it is all right to have money . . .'

'Compulsory, I can tell you . . .'

'. . . but not to have an interest in making it from something useful.' She turned round towards me and smiled, sadly. 'It's just like us here. We sell pictures and buy bonds, but we don't make anything that anybody could possible want. Nobody will remember us once we're gone. We didn't even contribute to the new *asilo*, John said it was nothing to do with us.'

'There's Davy. He'll be useful to somebody one day, won't you, Davy?'

The boy looked at me and then his mother. 'Yes,' he said at length and with some hesitation.

'You're going to be a watchmaker, aren't you?'

'A watchmaker?' This seemed eccentric even by Chadwick standards.

She turned squarely on me once again. 'Yes, why not? John doesn't think it's worth sending him to school in England. I agree and anyway our friend from Zürich, Jakob Hoffmann, wants Davy to be his *Lehrling*, you know, apprentice.'

'You said I don't have to be lehrling,' Davy had sprung up and now gripped his mother's smock.

'No, no, Davy. Not for years and years, or never, if you don't want to be. But I could come too, and we could live by the lake or in the big hotel with the passages, all by ourselves. And we'll see Onkel Jakob, who you like.'

Davy still looked doubtful.

'And Oriana is coming to lunch. You'll like that.'

Davy wriggled and ran back to the bed.

'Who is coming to lunch, Dawn? I never know what's going on in this house.'

'Braggiotti, of course, if the aeroplane can land in this weather. Giuseppe's picking him up at Capodichino. And you and John and Davy. And Amina when she's finished. And Franco Crespi, who sold the villa to my father, who's very nice but talks rather a lot. And Amina's brother, Giovanni, who's the grave-digger. He's not very bright, poor thing, and gets a bit plastered and then disappears for days on end and so we have to keep an eye on him. But so nice, and he's just lost his mother, so he's come to live with us. And Giuseppe, of course, who does the difficult jobs in the house and garden because John isn't very handy, as it were.'

'All together. Not very Newmarket.'

'Oh no, you don't understand. My father always had everybody together. Nobody in Italy minds social distinctions, or not much. Franco may go on about his family all the time but he still sits down with poor bonkers Giovanni.' She turned full round again, and sighed. 'Ah, Willie, I do love Italy. I could only ever live here, at Villa Crespi.'

'But who's this Oriana?'

'Franco's daughter. We were at school together and she's Davy's godmother. She's dynamite, isn't she, Davy?' She pointed the brush sternly at us both. 'Now there isn't going to be any kissy-kissy at lunch, is there?'

'No. No kissy-kissy with Oriana.' Davy sprung up and ran round the room, evidently much upset by the prospect.

'Now, now, don't worry, Dave. Dawn, give the poor boy a chance.'

'She is rather glamorous, you know. She has her own dress shop in Capri.'

'Nobody would look at her in this house, would they, Dave?'

'Oh what bosh.' She turned back, flustered, to the easel.

We were rescued by the sound of shouting.

'We're here! In the tower! And Davy, too!'

Chadwick was panting as he came through the door. He was wearing a dripping mackintosh and carrying a bottle of Carpano and a glass. 'What are you all doing up here? Your guests will be here in an hour.'

Dawn put her hands on her hips and laughed. 'We'd better buck up then, better hadn't we?'

Chadwick looked at me carefully and then took a large, wet roll of money out of his pocket. He handed it to Dawn but it was intercepted from her distracted fingers by Davy, who took the notes back to the bed for examination.

'He wouldn't take it?'

'As I said he wouldn't, if you remember, Dawn.'

'Bribe not big enough, old boy?' I said.

'It's nothing to do with you, Willie. It's nothing to do with us, for that matter.'

'Yes, it jolly well is.'

'My dear Dawn, by no stretch of definition could Amina's mother be considered a member of my household and my responsibility. Drunken bitch.'

'Well Amina is and Giovanni almost. If you don't do something about it, I shall, even if I have to dig the grave myself.'

Chadwick glared at her. 'Perhaps your son will help me.'

He strode to the bed, picked up Davy roughly by the arm and dragged him, shouting and showering bank notes, from the room. The door swung and slammed. Dawn looked after them with an expression of weariness.

'Dawn, for God's sake, what's happening? Nobody ever explains anything in this house.'

31

'It's so stupid I could scream. Poor Amina's mother died on Thursday, or at least she was found then by a hunter just below the Tiberio. The priest says it is suicide and so she can't be buried with everybody else. Giovanni's beside himself. John was going to offer a donation. They're collecting for a new garment for the saint we have here. But it doesn't seem to have worked. We have to do something. You know, they like to put them straight in here.'

'Can't Giovanni do it himself? It's his department, isn't it?'

'Yes, yes. Giovanni can bury her, but he needs somebody to read the service because he can't read.'

'Would John be that much better?'

'Well, somebody's go to do it.'

She spoke sharply and, as if to dull her sharpness, or to divert it from me, she bent to pick up a ten-thousand lire note. I knelt down to help her but she stood up and returned to her easel.

I looked at her back for a moment: 'What was the old dear doing up at the Tiberio anyway? That's Davy's place, isn't it, up on the hill?'

'Yes. Oh yes, I've brought that flower book up for you. Only, you promise you'll put it back on the table in the library, not in the shelves. It's more than my life's worth.'

'I'll look at it after lunch.'

'I fear it might not be that sort of lunch.'

I looked at her, but again she turned away.

The Crespis arrived first. Dawn opened the front door to them, then went off with their dripping things. They were left to me in the library. They ignored the Antinori champagne that had been put out and poured themselves brown whiskies, which I filled at intervals.

They were a striking pair. Crespi was none other than my learned stationer. He must have been about sixty; but he strode across the saloon with vigour and his hair, which formed a widow's peak over his forehead, was quite black.

He looked a little like a genial vampire. I remembered that he had once owned the house and expected that his manner would turn proprietorial; that he would walk round the room, clicking his tongue at the dirt and the patches of damp on the ceiling. But he sat still, alert and relaxed, always a guest. He spoke beautiful English, lisping his rs like a nineteenth-century guardsman. He was very likeable.

His daughter, too, was dark but taller than he and very slim; and whereas his suit had a greenish tinge in the watery light, she was a splash of new shop colours: blue jeans, a pink jumper and huge earrings of yellow paste. When I began to speak of the weather, she cut me off at once, established my origins and profession, and then was away, quizzing me about people and things in every city I had visited. She knew everybody of wealth and note, and her questions seemed but the tips of icebergs of accurate and fresh gossip. Restaurants, shops, a certain view across the Golden Horn; I had only to claim acquaintance to confirm her brilliant and worldly picture. The presence of her father pricked my conscience.

'*Marchesa*, I scarcely know these people.'

'Not *marchesa*, Oriana, like my shop.'

'Mr Nelson,' her father said. 'You must understand that Oriana cares only for her business. She is a Crespi as much as I.'

'Mrs Chadwick pines for the family brick company,' I said.

'But alas, her father was no businessman.'

'And what of your own father, sir?'

Oriana laughed: a short, quick ripple of sound, that stopped almost as soon as it had started, as if a door had swung open and shut on a party. Crespi looked at me curiously. I might have displayed a quirk of manners that intrigued him but he carried on: 'You are observant. My father was a Crespi aberration. He was an engineer and was intoxicated by the Futurists, or rather by Marinetti, with whom he lunched once at Capri. The house, the plasterwork on the tower, are the result of that fateful lunch. He interested himself in aviation. He became a supporter of Mussolini and took part in the march on Rome on a motorbicycle of his own design. During the depression, he tried to employ the village in excavating the Tiberio. He was a socialist, or rather a fascist, but far more a man without any sense of proportion, Mr Nelson. He constructed a funicular. The geology was unfriendly. Funds ran out. It is for my darling Oriana,' he said, gesturing gallantly at his daughter, 'to restore through commerce what was squandered through engineering.'

'And you shall help me, Willie.' She turned and interrogated me about my job. She took me apart, reconstructed me as a successful banker, then set me to work for her. I found myself promising her every sort of financial service, as if the City were as much in the palm of my hand as evidently Capri was in hers. Crespi had left us. Having asked my permission, he was now looking at the books and our conversation was accompanied by a lisping recitation. I felt Oriana was squeezing me to nothing. I tried to change the subject, and to involve her father, but she was single-minded. I began avoiding her gaze.

It was only when the subject of the stock market came up, and I had promised to underwrite Oriana's introduction in London, that Crespi looked up from his reading—it was Swinburne—and walked over to his daughter.

'Ah, capitalism, Mr Nelson. You would abandon my daughter to the beast.'

'It's the best system we have, isn't it?'

'Are you sure? Our Florentine cousins knew they were nurturing a beast. Could they have known the beast would slip every leash: the discipline of the values of the Ancient World, the loyalty to family and village and craft, the respect for the poor man as image of Christ? And you would take my Oriana to the *borsa* and abandon her to the beast?'

'I love that beast,' said Oriana.

'That will help you not at all. Capitalism ignores such sentiment.' He paused, and dropped his declamatory manner for something more humble and questioning. 'But what is happening in the *borsa*? Every day the index falls and falls. I sniff conspiracy.'

'I'm sorry, sir, I'm not up to date. But Mr Braggiotti from Milan is coming to lunch.'

'Aha, my friend Braggiotti will explain all.'

Dawn was in the doorway. 'Franco, Oriana, I'm so sorry. Everybody's late. I think we must start. Otherwise, the food will be nastier even than usual.'

'Oh come now, signora. It will be worthy of this house.'

We traipsed downstairs.

I had expected rissoles and steamed pudding. I found a feast: veal in tunny-fish, raw and cooked ham, piles of inshore fishes cooked in breadcrumbs, small pizzas of every description, anchovy *crostini* and a great bowl of pasta done in cuttlefish ink. We arranged ourselves round Dawn at the table, but the doorbell rang and went on ringing until Amina had laboured out from somwhere to answer it; and, in a little while, Guiseppe came in with a nervous, small man, both fitted out in dark suits. They were followed by three dirty figures.

'Davy, what have you been doing? Go with Amina and wash, this instant. John, how could you take him with you? Welcome, Giovanni. And Dr Braggiotti. I'm so sorry, please sit down, we haven't started.'

The situation would not arrange itself. Davy's mackintosh was no longer red, but black, his hair was wet and his face and knees muddy. He was bursting with laughter. Chadwick himself was just as wet. Only Giovanni, standing shyly in the door with his cap by his side, was clean. His face was quite blank, as if it had never been ruffled by care. The others looked on with interest and, in the case of the Crespis, solicitude; Braggiotti had found a seat and was deciding which leg to cross on which; and Giuseppe was standing, a picture of good tailoring, by the sideboard.

Dawn tried again. 'Now the burial party must go and wash. I'm not having you lot spoiling our lunch when Dr Braggiotti has come all the way. I'm so sorry, Franco, Oriana, but they had to go to a funeral.'

Crespi's handsome face twisted in alarm. 'I'm sorry, signora. We should not have come, if we had known. Please accept, from the marchesa and your old friend, the most distinguished sympathies.'

'For an intelligent man, Franco, you talk a great deal of rubbish,' Chadwick shouted from the top of the table. 'It was only Amina's mother.' He seemed to have no urge to wash. Instead, he was opening bottles of wine from a group in front of the gas fire.

'Rubbish,' said Davy, who was picking at the food on the sideboard.

Crespi's eyes sought out Amina to console. She was now serving the food and shrieking with laughter at Chadwick's sally.

Dawn was smiling. She had surrendered. 'Even so, John, you shouldn't have taken Davy with you. Did the *parroco* see you?'

'Of course he saw us. He stood under the porch, bawling about the police and injunctions and firing old dippy here. In fact, he should be grateful to have anyone to send the old lady on her last journey. It was,' he said, drawing a cork for emphasis, 'a triumph of co-operation.'

'Is there a strike?' For once, Oriana was at a loss.

'No, but Oriana, that awful Don Ambrosiano wouldn't let her be buried in the consecrated ground because he said she had killed herself. It's not true. We just had to help.'

'She was, my dear Oriana, a member of my extended household,' said Chadwick, pacing the length of the table. 'I make no distinction between my servants' families and my own, or indeed between my wife and child and myself. We stand and fall together.'

'Very Italian,' said Crespi, clapping his hands together. 'You must understand, Mr Nelson, that Italy is a country of public penury and private self-reliance. Many anglo-saxons, though I am sure not somebody as well travelled as yourself, believe that Italy is as feckless as its bankrupt institutions, among which, I fear, I must include our mother Church. This is not the case.

'Imagine,' he said, addressing the whole table now, 'there were a crime in the village, which God forbid, a burglary or an abduction. Nobody would seek assistance from the police, least of all our ambitious Captain Olgiata. The police are political toys, as likely as not to be in collusion with the criminals. They are quite arbitrary. At times, you know, whole professions are arrested: footballers, or theatrical impresarios. Here, Mr Nelson, it is every man for himself and every family for itself which leads to all those evils that you know of, like the *camorra* and our refusal to pay taxes, but also to some goods. We help one another.'

'I helped,' said Davy, who had come between me and Oriana. 'I got in the hole and then Giovanni came down too and he had to lift me out again.'

'*Che orrore!*' Oriana said, throwing up her hands.

'Not at all, you silly woman,' Chadwick shouted down. 'It is a salutary lesson for a child. It is never too early for a child to learn that the grave holds no terror.'

'Not for the dead,' Crespi murmured. 'For nothing can be predicted of the dead without absurdity. But for their former dependants....' He bowed to the top of the table. Amina straightened suddenly, as if required to be solemn. Giovanni giggled.

'Have the Crespis in all their long existence never heard of life insurance?'

Chadwick's tone was so insolent that Crespi paused a moment. Braggiotti spoke for the first time. His voice was glum and this was accentuated by a small American accent. 'Insurance cannot buy holy ground or a place in heaven, John.'

I was startled by such an old-fashioned sentiment from the only metropolitan guest. Even Crespi seemed to regret his cleverness, for he looked down at his plate; but Chadwick raised his voice yet further.

'Who on earth cares? All your religion and philosophy will never bring the peace of mind I have bought by insuring my life. When I die, my beloved Dawn will receive a lump sum of a hundred million and an *annualità....*'

'Oh John, please spare us details all over again. And no more shouting. Noisy, aren't they, Davy? I hate general conversation, don't you, Franco?'

Dawn turned all her attention to her left-hand neighbour and general conversation was at an end. The seating plan made it a labour even for Chadwick and the marquis. Having sat down beside Dawn at one end before the arrival of the others, the Crespis and I were now marooned by several empty chairs from the burial party, the airport group and Amina and Giovanni, who sat some distance back from the table. These empty chairs were filled indiscriminately by Davy, so that whenever conversation flagged or moved away, he was a convenient address.

Not that many angels passed at Chadwick's end. From what I could hear, or see past the silver and through the smoke of Braggiotti's Tuscan cigars and the steam of damp and alcohol, they talked only on two topics; the drunkenness of Amina's mother and the imbecility of Giovanni.

Oriana and I were thrown together. She was changed. It may have been the oddity of the burial, but she had ceased to be the conversational steamroller I had found so alarming upstairs. She asked advice, rather than gave it. She was interested in my occupations. She questioned me about Istanbul and my other postings. She invited me to Capri, to see her shop. When she wanted a cigarette or the wine, which she drank in abundance, she touched my hand. I began to admire her short black hair and slim waist and had to resist the temptation to be suave.

People got up and left, and sat back down again. At times, Oriana and I were left alone at table. At times, Davy came between us, to show her things. She let him take off and play with her earrings.

Once, when I looked up, Giovanni was balancing a glass of wine on his head. A little later, Braggiotti was playing battleships with Davy, both sides cheating horribly. The afternoon was drifting away. Perhaps it was the fumes of drink, which Chadwick kept bringing in, or Oriana beside me, that made the eccentricity of the house seem not quaint but risky. I longed for Davy to finish his game and come between us, or Dawn order everybody out into the rain.

It seemed Crespi had had enough. Placing his hand on Dawn's arm and rapping his glass with a spoon, he addressed the table. 'Now tell us, dear Braggiotti, how it stands in the market. Is the small investor, the widow, the orphan, to be ruined?'

'No, no, *marchese*. A technical correction, merely. A technical correction.'

'But how technical? I imagine 1929 was technical in nature, as well. My dear Braggiotti, must I now fall on the charity of the state?'

'Yes,' shouted Chadwick. He was clearly drunk.

'The market was overbought,' Braggiotti continued in his mournful voice. 'You must understand, *marchese*, that a stock market on a price/earnings multiple of 120 is no longer cheap in international comparison.'

'I wouldn't buy Italy on a p/e of 1,' said Chadwick, squinting at Braggiotti, and then down the length of the table. 'Would you, Davy?'

'What is this pee? Davy and I do not understand. Please explain, Willie,' Oriana said.

'It's a way, Oriana, of valuing shares or markets. You divide the price....'

'I wouldn't bother explaining to her.'

'Oof,' said Oriana, but Davy had climbed up on her lap and she must have thought better of replying.

Braggiotti merely continued, 'And I must add, *marchese*,' he said, 'that we in Milan are mere infants playing with anglo-saxon adults. The settlement arrangements broke down during the bull market. Foreign investors could wait six, nine months for stock. They were locked in to a market they did not trust. It only required the fall of the coalition in Rome— a banal event for us Italians—to break the foreigners' patience. On Thursday evening, a large Boston fund telephoned Lamberti and told him to sell. On Friday morning, London was also selling.'

'And what does this mean for the ancient house of Crespi, Dr Braggiotti?'

'It means you're bust. We won't bail you out this time.'

'John, how dare you speak to Franco like that? How dare you?' Dawn was standing. She was pale with anger. I had never seen her angry before.

'Lamberti borrowed, of course, against stock that had not been delivered.' Braggiotti was speaking quietly at the table. I don't think he could see that both Dawn and Chadwick were standing. 'It was common practice, because of the settlement delays. Only the market has fallen so far that the collateral is almost worthless. Rome will have to step in. I cannot see the Bank of Italy allowing a stockbroker to fail.'

'They're all bust, aren't they, Davy? The aircraft carrier's been hit. The game's over.'

'Stop it, will you!' Dawn was screaming now.

Chadwick stared at her, his eyes squinting. He took a step towards our end of the table, and then another.

'No.' Davy scrambled out of Oriana's arms and jumped up on the table. He tried to run towards Dawn but tripped over a huge, silver wine-cooler and fell on his knees. 'No, no, no, no,' he shrieked, his hands over his ears, his dirty face was streaked with tears. 'No, no, no, no, no.'

It was quiet. A drip fell into a water jug. I looked up at the ceiling and ran from the room.

I was too late. By the second landing, the carpet was drenched. The last flight of stairs was like a fish-ladder, the water pouring over the lip of each step in a broad stream. I could hear no sound of rain on the roof of the tower, but in the attic, every bucket so carefully placed that morning had overflowed. The sight made me angry and sad beyond words. I ran down to the library and saw pools of water on the carpet. I started pulling books out of the shelves and then stopped, disgusted, and trudged back up the stairs, thinking vaguely of saving Dawn's canvas; but when I opened the door, I saw Giovanni, standing with his back to me, staring at the picture.

'Giovanni, what are you doing? Get a mop, newspaper. The whole house is flooded. Get Giuseppe to turn off the power before we catch fire.'

40

He cannot have understood; but he turned and looked at me with his blank, unruffled face. Round his neck was Davy's drum and in each hand a drumstick. He looked at me, without appearing to see anything, and then trembled, dropping the sticks.

'Giovanni! Abbiamo fretta. Veramente.'

He scampered up to the attic behind me.

It seemed hours before we had restored order. Giovanni was a good worker and extremely strong: he could carry two full buckets in each hand and, later, in the library when we tackled the endangered bookcases, a shelf of books. At one stage, Giuseppe looked in on our work but, as I expected from his fine clothes, took no part. He stuck to the electricals, bringing up torches and lamps for us to work by. Dawn stood a moment on the step outside the attic. She was holding Davy by the arm. He was white with exhaustion or unhappiness. I sloshed across the room and squatted down beside him, but he turned, hiding his face in Dawn's dress.

'I'm putting this one to bed. He's finished, poor fellow.'

'Poor Dawn,' I got to my feet but she, too, turned away.

'Oh, don't worry, it always happens. Everybody gets over-excited about nothing, or at least we adults do.'

'Dawn, can't I do something? I mean, can you really go on like this?'

She seemed on the point of tears, but shook herself, like a dog after a bath, and smiled. 'They're going for a walk now it's cleared up a bit. To the lighthouse. John's gone to lie down. He's exhausted, what with the funeral and everything. Will you go with them?'

'Shouldn't I continue with the defences? There's still a lot to do in the library.'

'Just go, please.'

I must have looked horrified because she reached out and touched my chest. 'Willie, I'm sorry, I mean that Giovanni will do it. It's happened before. Every time it rains, in fact. Giuseppe says we should keep the lights off for a bit, so take care.'

There was nothing to be done with her. I crept down

slowly, but not slowly enough. I landed with a bump on the landing. The next flight I negotiated safely to the bottom but, thinking there was another step when there was none, fell forward, reached out, caught the base of a picture, snapped its wire and fell on my right side, the picture held triumphantly in the air. I leant it, unbroken, against the wall and crawled to the back door on all fours.

In the passage by the back door, I heard Crespi's voice. 'But, my dear Dr Braggiotti, don't you love the clash of male minds?'

'I would call that all-out war,' said Braggiotti grimly.

A ripple of laughter discovered Oriana.

'What are you doing down there, Willie?' She gave me a hand, which I took and kept.

'Mr Nelson, you have found us, at last. I was saying to Dr Braggiotti that the fierce exchanges over the table do not amount to anything: where friendship is said to subsist, as it does between our two families, courtesy is mere super-structure. But let us go to the lighthouse. It is five by the clock. Are you ready, Oriana?'

Her touch filled me with sweetness. As we came out into the damp air, I saw a scrap of blue sky on my left. But try as I might, I was separated from Oriana. When I lagged to allow her to catch up, so the marquis quickened, dragging his daughter with him and pointing facetiously at the plants in the ugly roadside gardens. Her back trembled, as if with laughter.

'Bad luck, my friend,' Braggiotti said, as we watched the Crespis stride on, he in a transparent mackintosh and evidently a little drunk, she matching his step, her shoulders still shaking.

I did not like the subject and changed it. 'It's pretty bad in the *borsa*, isn't it, Dr Braggiotti?'

He looked at me impatiently. 'The Consob has insisted on immediate settlement. Account trading is outlawed. Every transaction must be cash. The whole of Milan has borrowed against shares it does not yet own and which it can only sell for a fraction of the price when it does own them. The bankers

42

are baying for cash.' He laughed drily. 'And nobody has any cash.'

'Will Lamberti and the others go under?'

'Of course. They're rubbing their hands in Rome. Teach Milan a lesson, why not?'

'And Mr Chadwick?'

He stopped. 'Young man, why don't you talk with the *marchesa*?'

We re-arranged ourselves.

'Meanie,' I said, as Oriana and I slipped back.

She laughed. 'My father is a little cross with Braggiotti. I was doing as a daughter should.'

'Is your father really ruined?'

'Gracious, no. He has 50 Fiat savings shares and I bought him those. He likes to dramatise. And he's worried about John Chadwick, I think.'

'So am I.'

'Ah, he has Dawn to look after him.'

'I know, but God knows why she stays with him.'

'Willie, you are a big fool.' She took three quick steps and left me standing.

I ran down to catch up with her, on tiptoe lest I alert the two men. I could see their two backs, in mackintosh and green loden, swaying gently as they descended the road towards the lighthouse.

'I'm sorry, Oriana. I'm not so great at talking to women.'

'Oof!' She relented and slowed down. 'How can you know why one person stays with another person? English.' She smiled and gave me her arm.

'I can't, of course. But he's falling to bits, just living off Dawn's money, with nothing to occupy him. Can't you see how destructive it is?'

'Oh goodness, what does it matter? It doesn't amount to anything, you know. My father's right. It was just like this when Geoffrey—Dawn's father—was alive and Dawn and I were young.'

'But did the old man scream like that?'

'Oh yes, much worse. Dawn and I were terrified.'

I was looking at the ground, at a puddle of rain, and in it a corner of blue sky. And I remembered something from my last visit, as a bright day in winter brings a sudden intimation of midsummer. I remembered Dawn seated across from me, at a table we had under the almond tree by the kitchen, at the end of lunch. I was smoking and she reached across and took a cigarette from the packet and held it delicately between the thumb and forefinger of her left hand. And I heard a shout, more desperate than commanding after its journey through doors and along passages. Dawn stubbed the cigarette out. We both stood up.

'Willie! Are you listening?'

'Yes, sorry, Oriana.'

'It's just a game, for themselves or for visitors. Can't you see? There's nothing else to do. Of course, Dawn ought to have a business like mine.' She stopped and turned on me. 'Why don't you come to Capri, Willie? We would have fun.'

'Now?'

The memory flickered to life. I could taste the wine like pepper in my mouth. I had not drunk wine since then. And there was a fleeting smell, of fruit and dust, and the smell of the book in my hand.

'Oh all right, after Christmas, with your Dawn. But then maybe I won't like you so much and I won't be drunk.'

She strode off again, but I caught her arm. My mouth was dry and my legs felt weak.

'Shall we go up here, Oriana?' We had stopped at the turning to Davy's place.

'Do you want to make love with me, Willie?'

'Yes, please.'

'Let's find somewhere dry.'

We walked off the road, and through the houses, stopped and kissed. Her mouth, her tongue, her slim waist, her small bosom, the sweetness and novelty of her astonished me. She was so bonny.

'Not here, my *cavaliere*. The villa people can see us.'

'No. I mean there's a place up at the top, a garden with a summerhouse and an old pavement. I've been there before.'

'The Tiberio? So that's where you take your girls?'

'No. I mean, we can't go there. It's not safe. And there are hunters there at this time of year.'

She drew her head back and looked at me, not angrily, but in confusion. I could not stand the intimacy. I turned away.

'I'm sorry, Oriana, but we should get back.'

'Poor Willie. Maybe it's the old lady's ghost, haunting the place where she fell.'

She put her head against my shoulder. Through her black hair, I could see the lighthouse and the two men, walking back up the hill, their heads bent in conversation.

I heard her say, 'Let's join papa. You never know. You might get another chance.'

She skipped ahead of me down the path.

FIVE

by John Chadwick

I must now talk about William Nelson.

We shared rooms in Trinity. Even then, we had little in common. At that age, I was not aware of it. I arrived in Cambridge from my school in Bournemouth with my nature unmade. None of my family had been to university. I had no tastes and few habits. I had thought I was comfortably off. Nelson arrived with a large income, friends from school, a taste for alcohol and an interest in horses and riding. I had never met a public-schoolboy before, or heard the word charm.

Nelson's father was a partner at Cazenoves and owned houses in London and at Exning, near Newmarket. He was much more luxurious than rich. William could not distinguish the two. Although shy with strangers, he was generous with his money, not only to me, but to half Cambridge.

Visitors camped in our rooms. I often returned to find a ladies' shoe on the hearth-rug and once gave breakfast to a speechless, tousled girl. With William, I felt at the centre of Cambridge. Without him, I felt shut out of doors.

Our first year, he took me to point-to-points. He had a good mare, and often won. By the spring, he was spending half the week at Newmarket, at first in the company of jockeys and lads, and then with people from London. He took to drinking hard and could no longer make the weight, even on a steeplechaser.

His second year, he moved to a cottage I could not afford outside Cambridge. He tried to diet but it made him morose and drink more. The police found amphetamines at the cottage. A London doctor was bullied into testifying he had prescribed them for Nelson's weight. He bet more than he could afford. He was warned off Newmarket heath and nobody thought the worse of him. He became atrociously rude.

As my own character formed away from him, I became interested in my work. Nelson had no character, merely a set of tastes developed through indulgence. His defence against failure was not enterprise, but a literary self-pity. He was shy, as I say, and found it easier to assume a mask cut of Regency Newmarket than to compete for a place in the present. I saw that he surrounded himself with people, without distinction, for fear of boredom or solitude. Even I could no longer tell if he were patronising them. Perhaps he had come to doubt that the world must like and admire him. I saw he was frightened of his work. Only the dead languages he had learned at school scraped him a degree.

Nelson came into the City a year after I did. His father would not take him into Cazenoves. He was put in an American bank which placed an inflated value on a Cambridge degree. At first, we lunched together every month or so. I still thought my work important, and the charm of the place, and perhaps the language of money, intrigued him a little.

He must have spent all his own, for he was often short. He would take no hospitality from me. I saw that his generosity was merely an attempt to forestall criticism. Without money, he was obliged to compete. His public-school charm was no asset. His American colleagues thought him unserious. His modesty confused them. I think he asked for a posting abroad.

He went to Beirut in a lowly position. His superior had a family and was much away. An accident occurred. Dawn did not know what happened. It concerned the transfer of bullion from the bank vaults to a safer place outside the city. Nelson was recalled and transferred. He was foolish enough to have mastered Arabic. He passed through dim little postings: Istanbul, Sanaa, Cairo, Tehran.

Dawn continued to think of him. I did not. She said that his nerves had gone to pieces and he needed to settle down. She used to talk about pairing him with Crespi's daughter, an ignorant and vulgar woman but Dawn's friend. If this was a serious plan, it came to nothing. Though always on the point of breaking some journey at Naples, Nelson never came to Bocca d'Oro. The *marchesa* was always attached.

I did not stop to think why he came this time. He was Dawn's friend, like Hoffmann. I never interfered with her friends. How they had met, I did not know and did not seek to know. I knew she cared for him. She set him small tasks to do. He seemed to enjoy Davy's company. They went for walks together.

I should have been more cautious. At the moment Giuseppe let him out of the car, I could see he was on the verge of nervous collapse. He stared around him. He kept quizzing Dawn about an earlier visit. He had lost weight, no doubt because he had given up alcohol. He chain-smoked and had to be cajoled to bed. He jotted notes obsessively in an exercise book.

Unfortunately, I took little notice. I was pre-occupied with a new investment plan. For three years, our capital had earned splendid returns. Inflation had fallen and company profits had grown. But I suspected the markets were at or near a peak. Bond yields could fall no further and still leave a return, while the stock markets in London, New York and Tokyo were discounting dreams of prosperity.

I knew it was time to sell. I did not know what to buy. Only the Italian stock market was cheap. The coalition in Rome had been unable to pass a budget. Inflation was rising and the markets were nervous. I doubted that a nation whose invention defied the profligacy of its politicians would lag behind the rest of the world for ever. I sensed a buying opportunity. All I needed was expert advice.

I invited Emilio Braggiotti to lunch on 15 December. He was Geoffrey Durward's stockbroker and his partnership, Studio Braggiotti, is reputable by Milanese standards. I dislike the telephone and Braggiotti was always generous with his time.

The day started badly. Our servant's mother had died. The morning before, a hunter had found her body at the base of a cliff below a garden belonging to me. She had fallen from a height. She was known in Bocca d'Oro as a drunkard. I assumed she had slipped from the path. The police officer raised the question of suicide and the priest refused her burial. Her son, the sexton, who is an imbecile, was beside himself with grief and superstition. I felt bound to do something.

It rained all night. Clouds flooded the cliff and the roof sprung a leak. Giovanni, as the son is called, arrived in a state at nine a.m. and begged me to help him bury the old lady under cover of the rain. Finding Nelson wandering aimlessly, I put him to catching drips while I set off for the churchyard, Davy, who had an affection for the sexton, as children do with idiots, would not be left behind.

Dawn was foolish enough to invite the Crespis. The *marchese*, who is about sixty, is a bore even by the standards of the Italian nobility. He is poor but compensates with a wealth of pride in his family. He says it has borne arms since the Hohenstaufens. His reading is indiscriminate and he fancies himself a philosopher. The actual conditions of his life are squalid. He manages a general store that he calls a *cartoleria*, although it more resembles a junk-shop; and he lives alone above it with a 'Holy Family' that he attributes ludicrously to Ribera.

His wife abandoned him for life in Rome but he has the remains of an annuity originally issued by Dawn's father and paid by Dawn's trustees. He also receives money from his daughter who owns a boutique beside the Quississana in Capri. He commissioned Braggiotti to buy him penny stocks. He bought in when the market was high. Since then, it has fallen a quarter. I might have known that he would blame Braggiotti. I could not have known that he would arrive early and start drinking, as partial as any Italian to whisky. When we returned from the cemetery, accompanied by Braggiotti and his driver whom we met in the way, Crespi could scarcely stand.

His daughter drank as freely. She fell upon Nelson. Throughout lunch, she stared at him with enlarged eyes or laid her arm across his as she reached for the wine. The other guests were embarrassed. Davy was upset and confused. Crespi did not notice. I steered the conversation away from money and the markets, but this amateur would not be gainsaid. He pressed Braggiotti with questions. When these were politely answered, he turned to insults. There was a scene.

Reminded of his bad manners, Crespi apologised to me. The rain had stopped and I sent them all off to walk. Oriana and Nelson were enthusiastic. Braggiotti looked at me helplessly, but the day was already ruined. Our business would have to wait. They set off for the lighthouse at about six p.m. I went up to my dressing room to lie down, as I generally do in the afternoon, for Villa Crespi is an early-rising house. Dawn joined me and I slept.

I woke at seven p.m. Dawn was asleep beside me. It was dark outside our window. I was thirsty for water. When I tried the lights, they would not work. I thought it was a power cut, which is not unusual at that time of the day when electric lights and stoves are lit in the village. I keep a torch by my bed.

The first strange thing I noticed was on the landing. A picture had been taken off its hook and leaned carefully against the wall. It was one of Dawn's watercolours—of the stack of new books in the library—of value only to us. I supposed she had tired of it. She liked to demote her pictures when new ones seemed to her better. I proceeded down to the dining room. It was empty. Amina had washed up. The table, stripped of its cloth, was clear.

There was one curiosity. On the gas fire, which was still lit, there were two empty wine glasses. The rims were filthy with tobacco and scum. I supposed Oriana and Nelson had stolen back from their walk. The notion of their making love somewhere in the house infuriated me. Then I turned the torch on the table and saw it was empty. Every piece of silver that Durward or I had collected was gone. I lit the walls. A small Teniers had gone, leaving a dark patch behind, and the hanging was smeared with something dark. I went to the back door and found it off the latch. Cursing Nelson and

Oriana with all my breath. I ran upstairs but the big rooms seemed untouched. I stopped to calm myself outside the door to my bedroom.

I spoke softly to my wife. 'Dawn, you'd better get up and come downstairs. Something has happened.'

My face must still have shown alarm in the torchlight, for she sprang out of bed, her hair twisted and her face still creased from the pillow.

I said, 'In the dining room.'

She ran barefoot ahead of me.

Just inside the dining-room door, she stood still. I shone the torch slowly over the table, the wine glasses, the space where the Teniers had been and the stains on the walls.

'What's the matter? What's happened, John? Tell me.'

I shone the torch on the table again. Dawn began to sway. I reached out for her but she fell away from me. She raised her right hand to steady herself and touched the wall. She stood up, shook herself and looked at her hand. She screamed and was sick onto the carpet. The doorbell rang.

'Quick, into the kitchen! Wash it off. It'll come off. In water.' I picked her up, dropping the torch, and bundled her across the passage to the sink in the kitchen. Then I ran to the back door.

In the gloom outside, I could just make out Nelson. As he entered, I confess I balled my rage into a fist and hit him. He fell backwards against the door, shutting out the little light.

He cried, 'For God's sake, old boy. What are you doing? It's Willie.'

I hissed at him, 'How dare you treat my house like a whorehouse?' Or something like that. I tried to grip his wrist, but I missed in the darkness.

'What are you talking about? For God's sake, it's me.'

I think I said, 'Where is the bitch? Where have you put her?'

'What are you talking about? They've gone. Giuseppe picked them up. Braggiotti had to get to the airport.'

His fear calmed me down. I found his arm at last, and grasped it tightly. 'Come with me. See what you and your bitch have done.'

I walked him slowly to the kitchen. In the darkness, I could just see Dawn bent across the sink, her right hand in a jet of water from the tap. She was sobbing.

'Dawn, what has happened?' He made a movement towards her but I held him firmly.

'Willie. Upstairs.' She spoke through bubbles of tears and sick. 'Upstairs. Davy. Get him up. His clothes are there. Take him to Signora Nella's, at the restaurant. She'll know what to do. Don't come down here. Whatever you do. And John. Turn on the lights. Guiseppe turned them off at the mains.' She began to vomit again.

I let Nelson go and propelled him into the corridor. He dawdled but I pushed him forward. He made his way gingerly along the passage. I went back into the dining room and searched the floor till I found the torch. I heard the telephone receiver come off and then Dawn's voice. She was speaking German. She was evidently in shock.

She was saying, 'Please, Jakob. Come at once, yes, at once. Please, dear Jakob. Giuseppe will pick you up. But please come at once.'

I gently took away the telephone receiver. 'Don't bother me with Hoffmann, I need the police.'

Nelson was standing beside me. He was shivering. He said, 'He's not there, Dawn. The boy's not there.'

Dawn replaced the telephone and walked past us. I heard her walk down the corridor and then run. I heard her slip and fall on the stairs. Then I heard her screaming.

I turned to Nelson and hit him in the face.

SIX

by William Nelson

It was dark by the time I reached the villa and I was alone. I had not been able to face Oriana and the others and turned back to the village. In the bar, I surprised myself by ordering a *grappa*. I was cross for having cluttered my life, just at the moment when it seemed to be simplifying; and the taste of the *grappa*, the musty sweetness of it, revived chaotic memories. A firecracker in the square outside startled me and I looked up and saw a taxi crossing the square, with Giuseppe at the wheel and Crespi and the others squeezed into the back. I waited a moment, then set off back for the villa.

The lights in the house were still off. I rang the bell. There was no answer. I rang again. at length, the door opened a crack. I pushed forward through it but something hit me in the stomach and I sat down on the floor. I must have fallen back and closed the door for I could see nothing; but I could hear someone breathing heavily and muttering to himself.

'John, it's me, old boy. What's the matter?'

He lunged at me in the darkness and hit himself against the door. 'What have you done with her, the bitch?'

'John, it's only me. Have you gone off your rocker? Dawn was in the tower with Davy, putting him to bed.'

He lunged again and this time caught my wrist. He pulled himself towards me and whispered in my ear, so close I could smell the wine on his breath: 'Come with me. Come and see what you and the bitch have done.'

I felt badly frightened for Dawn. I ran fast down the passage to the bottom and then into the kitchen. There was a strange smell. In the faint light, I could see Dawn, in her nightgown, by the sink. She was cooling a burn on her right hand in running water. She was sobbing with the pain. She turned to me and said quietly and with difficulty, 'Go upstairs, Willie. Get Davy and take him to Amina's. No, not there, the house is closed for mourning. To Signora Nella's, the restaurant, you know. His clothes are on the chair. Don't come back down here.'

I understood, at last. I took a step towards Chadwick and said to him, quietly: 'So, you've done it at last, you bastard.'

'Just get Davy,' Chadwick screamed, pushing me out into the passage.

It has happened at last, I thought as I climbed the stairs. Thank God I'm here, I thought. I'll get Davy and then come back for her. They could stay at what's-her-name's and I can go to the Crespis or there might be a hotel. Hurry, I said, out loud.

I opened the door to Davy's room. It was like pitch inside, but I knew my way around it. On my right was the pile of toys and Dawn's easel. On my left was a chair. I crept between the two and came to the bed. Poor old Davy, I thought and leant down to kiss the head on the pillow. Then I straightened and struck a match.

The bed was empty. The sheet and the blankets had been gently turned back. I felt the sheet but there was no warmth in it. I looked for clothes on the chair but there were none. I forgot everything and ran down the wet stairs three at a time, tripping and sliding till I reached the bottom.

In the kitchen, Dawn was telephoning the police. Chadwick was trying to wrest the receiver from her. He had a torch with him which he shone full in my face.

'Leave her alone, Chadwick,' I said. 'You've really done it now. Your boy's gone.'

Something hit me square in the face and I fell; and as I fell, I saw a profusion of colours which arranged themselves, absurdly, into racing silks on the Heath. It was pleasant to watch the men and horses. Then I realised, with a quaint sense of loss, that I was not in England but lying on cold flags at the Villa Crespi.

When I opened my eyes, the light in the kitchen was on. The front of my coat was covered in blood, so I took it off.

The tap was still running in the sink. There was a small mirror above it. I saw that my lip was split and my teeth grated on something. As I rinsed my lip, it started bleeding again. I was dying for a drink.

I walked into the dining room. The gas-fire was on and the room smelt odd. A picture was missing from one wall. There was a dark patch where it used to hang. All round the room, the walls were smeared with excrement. Someone had been sick on the carpet. A person came in. It was Chadwick.

'We've been burgled and Davy has been taken.'

'I see,' I said.

'I think you should keep calm.'

'Yes.'

'You'd better not touch anything in here.'

'No.'

'Will you let the *carabinieri* in when they come? Take them to the library. Be quiet as I've put Dawn to bed with a Quanyl.'

'Is she all right?'

'Yes, yes.' He turned to go and then stopped. 'I suppose you left the door open on purpose.'

'No.'

'I'll talk to the *carabinieri*. I thought, oh I don't know. Oriana, I suppose. You seemed to like each other. I'm sorry for hitting you.'

'I'm not hurt.'

I went up to the library and sat down where I had sat before lunch. I could see my full ashtray and Oriana's glass. I took them both outside.

I thought: This is how they live. A curtain has blown away, or a shutter swung back, and I have seen a corner of their lives. It is not a game, as Oriana said, nor what I thought until a moment ago: a collection of arbitrary and trivial tyrannies like a royal family's exile. It is a house where frustration inhabits every cranny, a house teetering on the edge of violence or accident. I should have seen that Davy was not safe, that Dawn is not safe.

The doorbell rang.

There was just one officer, young and slim. He was wearing his black uniform and carried a smart, black leather handbag. As I let him in, he looked with interest at my broken mouth. I introduced myself and took him up to the library. He halted once on the stairs, to examine the picture I had knocked down, but he said nothing. Chadwick was already in the library, wearing his dressing gown and drinking whisky in messy gulps. I poured myself a glass.

The officer looked carefully round the room, sat down and started questioning Chadwick in Italian. Chadwick gave an account of the lunch as if it had been the last word in style. I could not believe my ears. He omitted the quarrel, but by then the Captain was impatiently pushing him on. He kept asking Chadwick the time when they came back from the cemetery, or sat down at table, or got up from the table. Chadwick's vague answers irritated both men.

'And you, Mr Nelson. What did you do after your excellent lunch?'

'I went up to the attic. You see, it was raining hard and the roof was leaking. I needed to empty the buckets.'

'How long did you do that?'

'Until Mrs Chadwick came up to put the child to bed.'

'And when, may I ask, was that?'

'About five o'clock. It was still light outside.'

'And then you went for your walk? At five o'clock?'

'Yes, with the *marchese* and *marchesa* Crespi and Dr Braggiotti from Milan.'

'And where did you go?'

I hesitated a moment, then said, 'To the lighthouse. On the way back, Giuseppe picked up the others in his taxi, to take them to Bocca d'Oro and Dr Braggiotti on to the airport.'

'So you came back alone.'

'Yes, after seven o'clock, I should think.'

'And what did you see in the house?'

'Well, I couldn't see anything. The lights were off.'

The officer turned to Chadwick. 'Why was that?'

'There was a power cut,' said Chadwick.

'No, no. Giuseppe turned the lights off. We were worried

that the rain would cause a short circuit.'

He looked at each of us, 'Am I to understand that the house was in darkness?'

'Yes.' We both spoke.

'I see. And I suppose that is how you cut your mouth. You fell over in the darkness.'

'No,' said Chadwick. 'I hit him. I was distressed, you understand.'

'And the broken picture on the stairs?'

'I slipped in the darkness and hit it.'

The officer got up from his chair. He looked at his watch. He seemed exasperated. 'Perhaps you will now show me the room where the boy slept and where you kept your silver.'

We walked up to the tower. The officer looked round the room, then went across to the bed and felt the sheet, as I had done. Then he ushered us out, closed the door and sealed it with some grey stuff he had in his bag. We walked down to the dining room. As he entered, he wrinkled his nose.

'Not unusual, unfortunately,' he said. 'What are those glasses?'

There were two glasses, dirty, sitting on the gas fire. I had not noticed them before.

'I don't know,' said Chadwick.

He took some polythene out of his handbag and wrapped up the glasses. He examined the gas fire carefully, then turned it off. He shooed us out and sealed the door.

'Please don't touch these doors. I'll return in the morning to speak to the signora. One more question, Mr Chadwick: do you have insurance?'

'For the silver and the pictures. You can't insure your children, Captain,' Chadwick said simply.

'Of course not. You have my sympathies. We will not permit this to happen. Good night.'

I showed him to the door. As we shook hands, he said, 'Perhaps you and Mr Chadwick should discuss matters a little. You have lost an hour.'

'What do you mean, Captain Olgiata?'

'A great deal can happen in an hour. Good night.'

'I still don't understand.'

The light flicked off. From the darkness, he said, 'Listen. I do not like you English. And I do not trust you.'

He receded down the drive.

I returned to the library. Chadwick had gone but I did not feel like sleeping. I drank some more whisky and, when I had finished the bottle, started another. I tried again to concentrate, this time on what Chadwick had said to Olgiata and on Olgiata's remark at the door. But my eyes kept closing and I saw pictures: Oriana in the muddy lane, Dawn weeping by the sink. I saw Davy walking determinedly somewhere in the darkness, out beyond the boundaries of the world he knew, and then, sitting, white with fear and loneliness, in a room full of men.

Guilt and fury overwhelmed me. I found myself standing up. I sat down but kept my eyes open, staring at the ceiling or taking notes for this diary, until I heard a car draw softly up. It was Giuseppe's taxi.

A large man got out and climbed the stairs in front of the hall window. He was so big he filled the landing, and Giuseppe had to stand on a lower step.

'Wait a moment,' I mouthed through the glass. 'I must do the alarm.'

When I had mastered the mechanism and drawn back the bolts, I saw he was an old man. White hair bristled on his face and from under a blue hat spotted with rain. He carried a thermos. I opened the door and introduced myself.

He sighed, opened the thermos, and poured himself a drink. It looked like neat gin. He poured himself another cup and said, 'I am Hoffmann. Mrs Chadwick asked me to come. Where is she?'

'Asleep, thank God.'

He looked round the room and peered into the library. 'What has happened?'

'The little boy has disappeared and the house has apparently been burgled.'

'Of course,' he said. 'Will you find me a room to sleep, if that is possible? We shall speak in the morning.'

He turned, took Giuseppe's hand, and put something in it. The boy put the money gently down on the window sill, saluted smartly and left.

SEVEN

by William Nelson

I woke, my eyes hurting from whisky. The hangover was familiar, but from several years back, and I thought I was at the villa on my first visit. The thought jarred and I woke a bit more. I kept my eyes closed, expecting to hear Davy's stifled laugh as he tiptoed towards my bed. Then I remembered there was no Davy and anxiety made me sit right up in bed. It felt like mid-morning but there was nobody about. I could not find Amina and burned my fingers making coffee.

The Chadwicks must have been keeping their room. There was no sign of Herr Hoffmann. The house was quiet except for the drip of rain on the roof and the perpetually chiming clocks. Occasionally the telephone rang once and then was answered.

I did not know where to sit. I walked up to the attic, and found myself standing before the door of the tower room. I returned to the kitchen but stopped at the dining room. Each time, as I stood distracted before a sealed door, the passage-light would flick off and I would have to feel my way along the walls, trembling at what my hand would touch. I could not sit on anything before examining it in the light. My shoes clattered horribly on the tiles of the hall. I took to tiptoeing.

I thought I would sit in the library, but the smell of my cigarettes the night before disgusted me. I started emptying my ashtrays and looked for a place to throw the empty whisky bottle. There was no wastepaper basket to be found and my journey to the kitchen stopped, once again, at the dining-room door. I tried the big library doors that led off to the Chadwicks' rooms. They were locked.

I sat down in the library. In the thin light, the room looked dirtier than ever. On my first visit, I know the house had seemed comfortable, inhabited, and not simply an apartment in which to sleep like the places I had rented or owned. How could I ever have found this room comfortable?

The silk cushions on the chairs were damp. The walls were hidden by bookcases which seemed never to have been touched; even the books that had got wet the day before had a permanent air where Giovanni had laid them to dry. Where there were no bookcases, ornaments made an impassable slalom of the floor: blackamoors and long-case clocks, tripods supporting lamps, cabinets of porcelain, watches, medals and miniatures, marooned in the curving room. There were no flowers in the vases. Malachite boxes held cigarettes, but they were stale and discoloured by damp. I turned on a dusty little computer and put in a disc, but it showed only the library catalogue. It was as if nobody but I had ever sat in the room, as if it were just a depository for objects to age, break, be liquidated or stolen, wasting assets like banknotes in a vault. The only thing of value had gone; and I found myself crying for Davy, because of my hangover.

I left the house and walked to Bocca d'Oro. I do not know what I wanted to do. I had reached the village before I realised it was raining and I had brought no coat. I stood in the little square, with its lopped plane trees, till a gaggle of boys rushed out from a doorway and threw a squib at my feet. In the barber's shop, I saw an old man having his white hair cut.

'Good morning, Herr Hoffmann.' I sat down against the wall and picked up a magazine. On the table was Hoffmann's open thermos flask. It smelled of water, not gin.

'Good morning, Mr Nelson. I have always my hair cut here, when I come. I hope you slept well.'

'Not really.'

'Naturally not.'

The barber seemed unable to speak. He was dancing in front of the mirror, cutting air and pointing drastically at Herr Hoffmann's shaggy head. Herr Hoffman patted his hair gently, then nodded in an exaggerated manner, and stood up. 'He cannot speak, cannot hear, good man. That is why I telephone from here.' He lifted an imaginary receiver to his ear and the barber, smiling proudly in recognition, gestured to a telephone on the wall.

'Why not telephone from the villa? Isn't that rather easier, Herr Hoffmann?'

He pulled from his trouser pocket a purse, which was stuffed with *gettoni*. 'I think not. Mr Chadwick is thrifty about telephone calls, just like my old friend Mr Durward.'

The mute barber was now making signs at me. To avoid hearing the telephone call, which was in German, I let him cut my hair.

Herr Hoffmann appeared in the mirror. 'Let us have lunch together down here. It's better not to return to the villa yet. I know a good restaurant, a very good restaurant.'

We emerged from the shop, but Herr Hoffmann had scarcely taken a step before he stopped before the next-door building, a dirty, small, orange-painted house with its steel blinds pulled down. On the door, there was a mourning poster, such as are common in Italy, with a blurred photograph of a group of women, one of them highlighted in ink, and beneath it a black cross. Hoffmann looked at it a moment and then turned his head, as if listening, before setting off as slowly as before. He led me through the rain into back streets that I had not seen before and stopped at a poor little house with its shutters closed. He knocked gently.

'I think it's closed, Herr Hoffmann.'

'Nothing is closed in Italy.'

A woman came to the door. She was wearing an apron. She looked at Herr Hoffmann and then, smiling, at me. He put his hands together as if in prayer, bowed, and asked if we might have lunch.

The woman shook her head and let us in. No, it was impossible. It was winter-time and they had nothing; only pasta really, and some *crostini* and two partridges that her son had shot the day before, but no fish and no salad, only some artichokes and some ham sent down from the Emilia and only their own wine and coffee would have to come from the bar.

I glanced around the small dining room and saw that I had

been there in 1978, with Dawn, with her father once, to repay his hospitality. I must have entered by another door that year.

The lady turned to me. 'It is a long time, professor.'

'Yes, a long time, signora. But here I am again.'

At the far end of the room, the family was having its own lunch. They stood up and the man of the house invited us to join their table, evicting his children. Herr Hoffmann declined politely and sought a table at the other end of the room. The lady immediately brought a jug of water which Hoffmann downed thirstily.

'It is impolite,' he said. 'But we must talk. I do not talk to Mrs Chadwick yet and so I will talk to you. About the boy.'

'Have you spoken to Chadwick?'

'He is busy. First, with the police and then with the insurance and then, who knows, the newspapers. By this evening, the village will know and the good people will come up to see.'

'But Herr Hoffmann, who are you?'

'I was Mr Durward's friend. And now I am Mrs Chadwick's trustee. I am Davy's godfather, though only a Jewish one.' He laughed loudly and abruptly, and I smelt his bad breath for the first time.

'In that case, Herr Hoffmann, I shall tell you all I know.'

I told my story as I have written it here. When I came to describe the lunch at the villa, he again burst out laughing.

'It was not funny.'

'I know, I know. Apology. But it is just like the old days, the days of Geoffrey Durward. How strange that husband has come to resemble father.'

'What?'

'You see, Mr Durward was always worried about his capital. Even the day he died, he was worrying about his capital. He was never poor, you see.'

'Were you ever poor, Herr Hoffmann?' Enfeebled by hangover, I was already a little drunk; and I was irritated by his obliqueness.

'Yes, young man, I was, during the war. Like everybody.

63

How old are you?'

'I'm thirty. Half my life is gone. I wonder sometimes if I have lived that half at all. I have forgotten almost everything.'

'Yes, the first half is the worst and I tried to forget it. I get older and I remember more and more. Have you heard of Theresienstadt in Boehmen?'

'I'm afraid I have. I'm sorry....'

'It was good training. For the second half. You sit and wait, with your friends, some in comfort, most in misery. Then one day, they are no longer there and someone says they went to Palestine. Or Shanghai. But they did not go to Palestine or Shanghai. A postcard comes from Birkenau. Do you know what Birkenau is?'

'I'm sorry, Herr Hoffmann. I didn't want to bring back painful memories.' I was desperately embarrassed.

'Don't worry. My family went to Birkenau. I went to Zürich.' He laughed so much that he had to take gulps from his water glass. 'Mr Durward kidnapped me in Vienna. Otherwise, I might be a high functionary in the Czechoslovakian Party.'

I tried to make the subject harmless. 'Did you go to Palestine? I mean, after it was all over. To Israel?'

'Heavens, no. Is it not better to live in Switzerland and think of Palestine, than live in Palestine and dream, oh dear, of Zürich?' He laughed again and his breath engulfed me.

'But after all that ...'

The proprietor's daughter delivered our coffee, on a tray brought from the bar. He smiled at her and patted her hand. 'I remember my youth time very much now. But enough of all this. Go on with your story.'

I told him of the leaking roof, and the walk, and my return. When I told him of the fight in the dark passage by the back door and the burn on Dawn's hand, he raised his eyebrows but said nothing. I described the police officer and our conversation in the library. When I finished, he turned and asked our hostess for *grappa*, for me, and another jug of water.

'I think you have been by Chadwicks before,' he said at length.

'Yes. How did you know?'

'Ach, you talk as if you are more than a guest at that house. And the housewife here knows you. When was your visit?'

'In 1978. In April.'

Hoffmann looked sharply at me. 'How can that be? The old man was still alive.'

'Yes. I didn't see him much. I wasn't very well at the time. I'd been living in Turkey and there was trouble, civil war almost. I came to rest.'

Hoffmann took no notice. 'But he let you stay in the house, with Mrs Chadwick, with Dawn, as she was?'

'Yes, of course.' Hoffmann's irrelevance was getting on my nerves. 'I read to him. Share prices from the paper and memoirs, I think. Cardinal Newman, perhaps. I remember very little from that time. My aircraft was hijacked. I work for an American bank. It was a bad time for me, you can imagine.'

But Hoffmann was unstoppable. 'And you do not like Mr Chadwick.'

'Oh for God's sake. Even you can see what he's doing to his wife. And the child. I told you what happened at lunch yesterday.'

'You think he treats Mrs Chadwick badly? Tell me what you know of him.'

It was my turn to be obtuse. 'Well, his grandfather invented the steak knife. His father worked in insurance. . . .'

'Excuse me, but I did not ask about his parents. What do you know of Mr Chadwick?'

I began again, wearily. 'We were friends at Cambridge University. We shared rooms. He was hard-working. He played bridge, very well. After his degree, he went to work in a stockbroking firm in the City of London. I met him sometimes there, although we were no longer friends. After two years, he was obliged to resign, just before he married Dawn, Mrs Chadwick.'

'And why? Why did he resign?'

'We call it insider trading. In those days, it was not a crime.

Some say it is not a crime now. He was buying shares p.a., I mean for his own personal account, on secret information he had from his colleagues. It was not much, maybe £10,000, but his senior partner found out and he was asked to leave.'

'And who knows this?'

'I do and a few others in the City. Mowbrays did not want a scandal.'

Herr Hoffmann laughed. I became aware, not for the first time, of his bulk in that small restaurant. 'I am an uneducated man. I know only to mend watches. But I feel things; and when I see something, a watch, maybe, or a picture, I do not think this is by so-and-so or what is the signature, but I try and feel it, feel if it is quality. That way I am often right. That is why I am talking to you.'

'But what's this got to do with Davy and the men who took him?'

'Don't you understand, Mr Nelson?'

'No, I do not.'

'It comes to me something ungenuine. Hijackings and stealing shares. Perhaps, Mr Nelson, you are the men. Or perhaps, you let in the *camorra* to take my godson.'

'You're mad, Hoffmann.'

He seemed to fill the whole table, big and canny and fetid. I stood up.

He laughed and drank some more water. He reduced in size and his pleasant face was covered in warmth. 'Now, don't worry. I am not always right. Come, let me invite you for lunch. As one gets older, it is more pleasure to be host than guest.'

We had to struggle back up through the rain. As we passed through the gates onto the gravel drive, we saw a crowd of people in front of the house. We quickened our pace and saw that they were nuns, black as ravens in their plastic mackintoshes. We passed them with greetings and one blessed us with a sign of her right hand. I looked up and saw that lights were on in the tower.

Amina was waiting in the doorway, smiling as ever through her gap teeth. It was as if nothing had happened.

The seal on the dining-room door was gone, and in the kitchen Dawn was seated, eating something. She had made a sort of sandwich out of dark chocolate and bread and was biting into it just as we entered.

'Oh Jakob,' she said, springing up. She hugged the old man tightly around the waist and laid her head on his chest. I turned away, embarrassed.

'Hello, Willie,' she said, at last disengaging herself. 'Did you have some lunch?'

'We went to Signora Nella's,' Hoffmann said.

'I'm so sorry, it's been mad all day. Even the sisters from Davy's *asilo* have been here.'

'Is there any news?' I was surprised by her equanimity.

'No. The police have been here all day. John's been dealing with them. They've put a tape recorder on the telephone, just in case. They think it may be a gang from Reggio. It's happened before.'

'You are brave, Dawn.' It seemed as if her day and night alone had washed her of her loss and fear.

'Well, what's the point of moping? John's gone to bed. He's exhausted, what with the police and the insurance man, and the telephone ringing and thinking every moment it will be them. Do you mind having dinner here on your own?'

'Oh, don't worry about us,' I was shocked by her high spirits.

'Oh Jakob, there's one thing. We can't find the infernal Giovanni.'

'The mad one?'

'Yes. He's supposed to be living here now because his mother's house is closed. Amina is terribly upset. She thinks he was so frightened by Don Ambrosiano and the whole business with the burial that he's gone off on one of his binges. She's been all round the village.'

'Does the captain know this?'

'Yes. There's a warrant for him, or whatever it's called. Poor Giovanni. He wouldn't harm anybody.'

Her cheerfulness fell away. Her face began to contract in tears. Hoffmann broke in suddenly. 'Perhaps, my dear Dawn,

I might see the room where it happened.'

'Yes, yes. Amina and I have cleaned for you.'

The dining room smelt strongly of disinfectant; but the marks on the walls and carpets were gone. As she entered, Dawn began to shiver again but Hoffmann put his arms round her shoulders and led her across to the bare patch on the far wall.

'The Dutch wedding?'

Dawn nodded.

'Well, they have judgment. 150,000 francs reserve. And the silver, too, I see. Where is the thing for putting bottles in?'

'The wine cooler. It's gone. But they left some things behind. Captain Olgiata found them this morning.'

She opened the two doors of the sideboard. Inside, pieces of silver had been stuffed in, anyhow. The railway train was there but was twisted from its carriages. A large salver had been badly dented.

'They must have left in a hurry,' she said, looking appealingly at Hoffmann.

'But you have not found the wine cooler?'

'No.'

'This may be good news,' he said with a deep sigh. 'These are professionals. They are not a gang from Reggio. They took only first-quality objects that are easy to sell: a fine picture by a prolific artist and a piece of silver that would be for you to identify. This is good news for young Davy.'

'Do you want to see upstairs, Jakob?'

The tower room was also tidy. The bed had been made and the floor swept. Hoffmann looked out of place, so large in that tiny room with its mad windows and circular floor. He picked up a book, stared at the spine a moment, put it down, knelt beside the pile of Davy's toys, raised himself up with difficulty, examined Dawn's canvas, then burst into tears.

He howled. His large head bowed and his face, with its white whiskers, seemed to crumple like paper. 'I brought him my watch instruments, my first set, for his Christmas,' he said. Dawn reached out and led him to the bed, where he sat down heavily. 'I wanted him to learn, as I did and Ariel after me.'

I could not look. I turned to stare at Dawn's canvas, struck once again by its beauty and accuracy. I looked at the pile of toys and then back at the canvas.

'Something's missing.'

'What? What do you mean, Willie?'

'Quick, come here. Look here. There's something missing.'

She glanced at the pile of toys and grasped it in an instant. 'The drum is gone. Davy's drum. Willie's drum. The drum, Jakob, that Willie brought back from Istanbul.'

Hoffmann got up and looked at the toys carefully. His tears had vanished as quickly as they had arrived. 'Perhaps, they weren't in so hurry.'

'I think they wanted him to have it. To keep him happy,' I said.

They both stared at me. Then Dawn came over and kissed me on the forehead. 'Clever Willie,' she said. 'My clever Willie.'

'Clever,' said Hoffmann. Then he turned away and said, 'You remember, my darling, that I wrote an inventory for you of the objects in the house. Can you find that for me?'

EIGHT

by John Chadwick

I did not sleep last night. Davy had been gone just a few hours. I needed to think and act quickly. Nobody else would, least of all the captain of the *carabinieri* who wasted two hours of my time that evening in irrelevant and suspicious questioning; not Dawn, breathing and turning heavily in her sleep, or her friend Hoffmann, who bustled into the house in the early hours of the morning; certainly not William Nelson. I was alone.

The rain dripped outside. I put from my mind all that I did not know; who they were, how many they were, how they had got in, where they had taken the boy, why they had taken him. I concentrated on what I did know.

I knew that they had come between six and seven p.m. I knew that at that time, I was in bed. That Dawn was also in bed, and the others walking to the lighthouse, fell into the category of speculation. I knew that the burglar alarm was off, because of the loss of power, and that I had found the back door open at just after seven p.m. I knew that my beloved son and two objects were missing: a Teniers oil of a wedding scene and a George II wine cooler. Other objects might be missing, but I knew about only these. There was no evidence of violence except the excrement on the walls of the dining room and a broken picture on the stairs.

I went into my dressing room and drew out Hoffmann's secret inventory. The objects were not the most valuable in the house, but they were precious. In 1978 Hoffmann valued the '*Nice Dutch Wedding*' at 70,000 francs and the '*Silver Bottle Barrel*' at 65,000 francs. Dutch seventeenth-century painting and Georgian silver had appreciated strongly in the interval. In an insurance valuation for the Creditanstalt, Hoffmann had written up the objects to a quarter of a million francs.

These were my facts. I began to make deductions. In taking the objects as well as the child, the thieves had acted unprofessionally. Fenced in Italy, the works of art would not raise much: fifty million lire, or perhaps a little more. For that sum, they had risked exposure for the much more serious crime of kidnapping. The objects had surely been photographed at some time and could be traced back to me if they came onto the market. It was a crass piece of greed, as unfathomable to me as the shit on the walls. The risk to Davy from such madmen was quite unquantifiable.

I was at a dead end. In order to plan, I had to assume that Davy's abductors were careful men. As the night progressed, I stayed with my facts, but re-arranged them. What if the filth on the walls were designed to terrify us? That was professional. And the picture and the silver were taken, not simply out of greed, but as part-and-parcel of Davy's abduction: to help provide me with the means of paying a ransom for him? For the works of art, I would receive a quarter of a million francs in insurance, or a quarter of a billion lire. I might be merely a means for a group of men to extort cash from the Creditanstalt.

The thieves could not know what I and one other person knew at that time: that for two years I had covered myself, Dawn and Davy against abduction. The other person was the director-general of the insurance subsidiary of the Creditanstalt.

I have always been intrigued by life insurance. It takes away the sharpness of death. My own policy will give me temporary immortality. Even after I die, Davy can draw capital from my grave. Two years ago, during a spate of kidnappings in Sardinia, I took the logical step of protecting each one of us from violence.

I had deposited the abduction policy along with other valuables at the Creditanstalt. It provided for cash payment up to one million dollars against a demand for ransom. The premium was by far my largest cash outgoing. I had always known the policy was cheap if it meant that the life of a member of my household would never be endangered by lack of funds. Last night, it kept me sane.

I knew that there was a risk that the police might hinder the payment of the ransom. The cover was illegal in both Italy and Switzerland. I was sure Olgiata would open our correspondence and follow our movements. It occurred to me that Davy's abductors might have reached the same conclusion. They would not contact me in person. They would use some other means.

Light was seeping through the curtains. I had left my four facts far behind in the small hours; but the chain of deduction was sound. I progressed carefully and without prejudice. I considered all the people around me. One of them, or more than one, might have conspired with Davy's abductors against me.

Giovanni, Amina and Giuseppe had ample opportunity to betray me. Amina and Giovanni knew the house inside out. Giuseppe I had often found on the roof, fixing a tile where it had come loose or shinning up through the tower-room window when Dawn had mislaid her back-door key. The Crespis, father and daughter, had lived in the house.

All were my dependants. It was quite illogical for any of them to seek to rob me. They were simply robbing their future pensions. A ransom may force me to mortgage the house and try to liquidate Dawn's trust. If I then declare us both bankrupt, we will not be liable for the servants' pensions or the Crespis' annuity. But last night, I did not credit any of them with such logic. I did not exclude them.

I considered Hoffmann. He knew the value of the objects taken and, worse, a great deal about Dawn's financial standing. I regretted that I had trusted him at our first meeting in Zürich. I regretted taking him on Dawn's valuation. As for Nelson, whose arrival had been so timely for Davy's disappearance, I knew nothing of his friendship with Dawn.

I abandoned this line of thought. I was becoming prey to distracting suspicions. I knew it was my own responsibility to defend my family. I had nobody to blame. I saw, too, that it would be to my benefit if any of these people were in collusion with Davy's abductors. He or she would contact me. I might find a note in my mackintosh pocket or between the pages of the newspaper. I needed only to wait.

Yet this all seemed melodramatic and amateurish. I reasoned as if I myself had abducted Davy. I would have contacted the Creditanstalt directly, or at least my financial adviser in Italy, Braggiotti. Keeping me informed through either channel seemed an altogether more professional approach. I rose and dressed as quickly as I could and left through the back door.

In the square, the bar had just opened. It was empty, but for the barman. Chairs were still stacked on tables. I ordered a *ramazotti* and took it to the telephone. I recognised this as risky. Davy had been gone at most eleven hours. I knew Olgiata, I did not credit him with the energy and resources in that time to put a tap on the local exchange serving Bocca d'Oro. What happened afterwards, whether he heard of the fact of the telephone call, did not matter.

Braggiotti was already in his office. He was taking selling orders from Japan, I explained what had occurred. He all but dropped the telephone in alarm. I knew he was thinking of his own situation. In other circumstances, I might have enjoyed preparing him for his police interview, which could only have been hours away at the furthest. When he had finished his futile consolation and promised all his help, I explained what I wanted him to do.

If they contacted him, he was to telephone me, using an ordinary stockbrokers' code such as we often used together. I also proposed a schedule of meetings at Capodichino, at the arrival of the evening flight from Milan, the particular day to be triggered by an element of the code. His is a quick mind and he had recovered. He said a telephone call would be safer and gave me a private number of his own, for use at a fixed time every two days.

My other request of Braggiotti was to telephone the Creditanstalt on a private number I gave him, along with the code name for my policy. He promised to pray for Davy, which surprised me, and then he hung up. As I left the bar, which was still empty but for the barman, I felt immeasurably relieved, I felt I had established an element of control, like regaining the lead in bridge.

I lay down in the bed for a while beside Dawn, The telephone started ringing at about nine o'clock. It did not stop all day. I took it into my dressing room and dealt with Crespi, who had rung to apologise for his rudeness at lunch. I listened carefully to his chatter but told him nothing. The police were not so discreet as I. The telephone calls followed in rapid order. Delegations of people, from Giuseppe's mother to the nuns from Davy's school, were knocking at the door to gawp.

Olgiata came early. He was accompanied by two detectives. He asked more of his pointless questions. He unsealed the two rooms, photographed them and dusted them for fingerprints, I would not let him speak to Dawn, who was still asleep. Nelson was nowhere to be found. Muttering, they left to interview the Crespis.

After they left, I settled down to wait. To still my nerves and pass the time, I started this record. I am short-sighted and do not take notes. When I need an aide-mémoire, I use a tape-recorder. I have filled one tape already, and hidden it in the secret drawer of old Durward's desk.

It is now evening. At four p.m., Dawn woke. She took a long time to struggle out of sleep. She was disoriented. I explained what had happened. She got up, dressed without speaking, and called down to Amina's room. I left her to start cleaning the house, for she needed something to do.

An hour later, Hoffmann and Nelson returned from a drunken lunch. I did not go down. I would have thrown them out of the house, had I not needed them.

At five-thirty p.m., I received the coded telephone message from Braggiotti. I left the house quietly by way of the upstairs hall door and telephoned the private number from the newsagent. He had received a telex. It was brief and in English. It said: 'Message one of three. Pls await instructions on delivery of stock. Regret cash settlement only. Regret delay will entail liquidation of position. Bestest.'

The vague message surprised the telex operator in the dealing room of Braggiotti's Milan office. She had taken it to him for clarification. He had checked the answerback in the directory and found it to be the PTT in Naples. When he got through to the post-office operator there, he learned that the message had been handed in, prepaid, the night before. He was still doubtful. I was not. I told him to do nothing and wait for the next message.

I have told nobody of this conversation, not even Dawn. I do not trust the police to help me and I will not help them. We have different aims. They wish to catch Davy's abductors and gaol them so that they cannot take another child. My aim is to restore Davy to his family at any cost except that of his own safety. Other children are of no concern to me.

I have taken the first steps to master the crisis. I am going to bed, to sleep, for the first time in two days.

NINE

by John Chadwick

In the early evening of 20 December—the day before yesterday—Braggiotti telephoned with his code. I dared not call back from the village, so I boarded the late bus to Naples and got off at a petrol station in Pozzuoli. Whether I was followed or not did not matter. The fact of my telephone call was nothing to its substance.

The message was again a telex, again in English. It said: 'Message two of three. Position to be liquidated. Short swfr 500,000 rpt swfr 500,000 a/c piccoloneu. Regrets.' Once again, the message had baffled Braggiotti's telex operator. Once again, he had found the answerback to be a public post office, this time in Zug. Braggiotti could make no sense of it, except its threatening tone.

I returned by bus, changing twice, and walking back the last mile along the promontory. It was dry and the sea was calm, but I was cold, I made Nella open the restaurant, drank a bottle of wine and ate a plate of anchovies, then went looking for Olgiata. He was playing billiards in the Scaline, and I drank beer with him for an hour. Then I walked home and lay down in my dressing room.

The message was difficult, I marshalled my facts. There were two statements in the message: that the transaction was to be called off and the sender lacked funds. The import haunted me throughout my long journey home. I had expected a precise demand for cash, a place to deposit it and a warning of the consequences of failure. Yet the message was numbered two of three. There had been no intervening telex. There had been no message but the telex marked one of three.

I read the message again. There was a precise demand, for

500,000 francs, a reference to an a/c, presumably account, and a warning. But they were back to front. When I rearranged them in the natural order, demand, account information then threat, the message became obvious and indiscreet. I breathed loudly in relief.

The telex contained two related pieces of information: a demand for 500,000 francs to be deposited in an account and a threat to do something if the demand were not met. Not fact, but reasonable assumption, was that the message came from the same source as the first: the message was numbered in the same way and had been sent from a PTT. The threat of liquidation was, equally plausibly, a threat to my son's life.

The message did not yet contain enough information on which to act; while the numbering of the message, two of three, made a long correspondence on detail improbable. The message must contain more information, perhaps in a coded form to confuse either Braggiotti or the financial police. I heard a sound.

Dawn was awake. She was crying in our room, as she does every night when she wakes up. I ration the Quanyl. I know that she looks forward all day to taking the pills. They are damaging her nerves. She veers between gaiety and inanition. Her memory is unreliable. She calls me Willie sometimes, or addresses me in German. I gave her one pill more. She held me gently till the drug took hold. Then I slipped away from her.

I returned to the second message. Where was the additional information? Who or where or what or how was piccoloneu? I went into the library and looked up the word. I repeated it in different accents. It sounded Turkish or Rumanian; but though the reference books had entries enough for piccolo, as meaning small in Italian, or a little pipe, or various slang words for a drink or a tip or a part of the body, there was nothing for the word itself. I tried abbreviations and then anagrams, arranging the letters in a circle like a commuter with *The Times* crossword puzzle. Then I broke up the word and looked at its parts: piccolo and neu.

Neu: noo, nyoo, neu as in French neuf, noy as in German.

Noy sounded familiar. Something noy. Something Noy with a capital. Haus Neu, Bankhaus Neu.

I halted. The money was to be deposited at an account piccolo at the Bank Neu. Or at the piccolo Bank Neu, the little bank Neu. I turned to a directory of world financial institutions. The library had never been so useful. Under Zürich, I found the Bank Neu, at an address in the Bahn-hofstrasse. It had no other branches in Zürich. I looked through the entries for every other financial centre, including Bahrain. There were correspondent banks in Chiasso, London, New York and Tokyo. There was no little Bank Neu.

I returned to my facts. The demand was for 500,000 francs to be deposited at the Bank Neu in the Bahnhofstrasse at an account piccolo or Piccolo with a capital. Who or what was piccolo?

It was simple now. Piccolo was the code name of a fiduciary account at Neu, just like my own coded account at the Creditanstalt. Piccolo meant little and referred to little Davy. This was supposition, but compelling supposition. I cursed the secretive Swiss, with their numbered and coded accounts, as I had once blessed them; but I recognised the elegance of the solution.

If I showed the telex to the police, or if they found it in transmission, they would have to apply to a Swiss court to gain access to the account. In the day or so it might take to gain even an injunction, the prudent men at Neu could eradicate every trace of it. I remembered my man at the Creditanstalt, his desk entirely clear of paper. The telex also implicated me. The mere suggestion of a transfer to Switzerland brought me into suspicion. It was an illogical demand unless I had my own account in Switzerland or planned to transfer funds from Italy. Both were illegal.

I was alone, as always. I did not underestimate the police. If I could decode the message in two hours after midnight, how much more quickly could skilled officers expert in the financial traffic through Milan? Braggiotti had been handed the telex at six p.m. It was urgent that he should set off for Zürich before the working day began.

He had the telexes, and my power of attorney identifying my account at the Creditanstalt and the associated insurance policy. Braggiotti's own reputation would soothe the Creditanstalt's qualms in making an advance and transfer to the Bank Neu. I did not hesitate to ring him at home. He was sleeping, but he is a professional and expected my call. I gave him the signal that I would telephone his secret number at six a.m.

I lay down in my clothes beside Dawn, who was now sleeping well. I set the alarm for five o'clock and had scarcely shut my eyes before it woke me. I knocked on Giuseppe's door in the village and he drove me to the north, to another petrol station. I checked that it was outside the Bocca d'Oro telephone exchange, I rang the private number. There was no answer. Braggiotti's office was silent. At his home, a distraught daughter told me he had left with the police an hour earlier.

I was alarmed, I assumed the police in Milan had intercepted the second message and made sense of it. By now, they could well have searched Braggiotti's office and found the first. I expected Olgiata at any moment. He must on no account find the tapes. I toyed with the idea of destroying them but rejected it. I would place them in the library stacks where they might not be found for weeks.

There was nothing on the seven o'clock news. At eight o'clock, the RAI had a long story. After the news item, there was an attempt at commentary by the station's financial correspondent. He dubbed it 'the Massacre of the Bourse'. At five a.m., the financial police made one of those mass raids that are such a glory of Italian justice: one year, it is opera-house directors, once the entire staff of the Bank of Italy. This time, it was stockbrokers.

The journalist had evidently been briefed by the police. He tried to explain what I already knew: that all the main brokerages were trying desperately to prop up share prices by buying in the market on credit from the banks. He said the raid was politically motivated and wandered into the maw of party politics, where he lost me. I was relieved. I knew there was safety for Braggiotti in numbers. Simply for the show of it, I rang his office and offered to contribute to his bail bond. I went back to thinking.

If Braggiotti could not go to Zürich to make the transfer to the Neu account, who could? There were three possibilities: I could go, I could delay until Braggiotti posted his bond and I could send another person.

I rejected the first two possibilities. It was out of the question for me to go. I was watched. A policeman waited in front of the villa gate. Delay was no alternative: if I delayed, I jeopardised Davy's release. I suspected that the transfer to the Neu account would trigger a third message, three of three, giving Davy's whereabouts. On Christmas Eve, the banks would close for two days and the transfer would be delayed. In the interval, ample time to search Braggiotti's premises, anything could go wrong. Delay was futile for another reason: even if Braggiotti were released quickly, which was likely on the precedent of the opera directors, he would be confined to Milan. There was no chance he or his confidential assistant could pass through the airport or across the land border to Switzerland. The attempt would merely confirm the suspicion of financial malpractice. Braggiotti would refuse to go.

I had no choice. I had to find somebody to visit Braggiotti in gaol, establish the whereabouts of the two telexes and take them, with my power of attorney, to Zürich. Whom could I trust?

The question disgusted me. I had never consciously trusted any person or institution. Unwittingly, I must have trusted somebody because Davy was gone. I was now forced to trust somebody else to bring him back.

Whom did I least distrust?

I ran down a list of Dawn's friends. Franco Crespi was congenitally indiscreet. His daughter was interfering and malicious. Hoffmann was a plausible go-between: a well-known, if tawdry, figure about Zürich and a customer at the Creditanstalt. But he was certainly not to be trusted. He had leached the Durwards, father and daughter, of their best property; and he knew the value of the pieces that were stolen, which brought him directly into suspicion. I would sooner have trusted Nelson.

Whom did I least distrust? I worried at the question for two hours. I thought I would rather send the barman from the Scaline than any of Dawn's friends. I would rather send Giovanni.

The idea brought my solution. I did not need to send one of Dawn's friends. I did not need to send a person of sophistication. My man at the Creditanstalt spoke Italian. Braggiotti spoke Italian. I would send Giuseppe.

I collected money from the desk and walked down to the village. The risk troubled me. I did not know that Giuseppe was not implicated. But I had given each person a weighting for risk and Giuseppe came out lowest. He was washing his taxi in the street. I asked him if he had a passport. He nodded and I explained his task there and then. He smiled at the responsibility entrusted him. He refused my million lire till I lost my temper. He left for the airport at once.

Yesterday passed slowly. I listened to the radio every hour but there was no news of Braggiotti. Through the wall of my dressing room, I could hear Dawn and Nelson giggling like children. They were decorating our Christmas crib, a marvellous thing made in the Black Forest in the eighteenth century and worth tens of thousands of francs. I hated to think of Nelson handling the carved figures in his clumsy fingers.

I came on Dawn later in her room. She was sitting cross-legged on her bed, wrapping a bottle of whisky for the marquis. I watched her for a while. Toys and books, scissors, tape, ribbon and paper covered her bed. I watched her bend over each completed package, writing a message on each. Her tongue was between her lips. She held the pen in her awkward way, between the thumb and forefinger of her left hand. I looked at the parcels that filled a laundry basket by the bed. To Davy with his mother's love. To Davy with love from Bot. To Davy love from Mina. To Davy love from Giuseppe. One had even been sent to the barber for signature, or rather a cross.

I sat down beside her and put my arm round her back. She smiled at me. She said, 'Will you help me put these under the crib? It's in the library. We've done it up for him.'

I said, as gently as I could, 'Why don't we put them in a drawer for the moment, why not? Until he's back.'

'He will be back, John, for Christmas, I know.'

It was no use. I carried the laundry basket into the library and upended it by the crib. By the time I returned, she was off on a new tack: to invite guests for dinner on Christmas Day. I objected patiently. I said I did not want strangers in the house again. I would not use the dining room again. She wept and kept silent for an hour, hunched over her trashy presents, till I said she could have whom she liked. I would not attend. She wept again. She said she would use the upstairs hall. I gave in.

I am now very alarmed about Dawn. She has few resources. She is not educated, except to speak languages. All her strength and will are dedicated to our household, and its embodiment in Davy. Even her painting is confined to the house.

I remember that when Davy ceased to depend on her entirely and put behind him his rages, we talked of having another baby: a girl preferably, but it would not matter greatly. The suggestion shocked Dawn. She seemed to be saying that a second child would dilute the love and care pledged to Davy. Aware this was nonsense but that our money, at least, was finite, I reluctantly agreed.

Davy's abduction is the one event most likely to destroy her. Only a jealous God could have devised it. I feared the discovery of his absence might overturn her mind. She survived. But each day that passes, I hear the sound of pieces falling.

Never a tidy woman, she has let herself go. She no longer brushes her hair. In the morning, I can see the effort with which she draws on a pair of stockings. But for Amina, who brings me a tray in my dressing room twice a day, I would starve. Far from helping me negotiate Davy's release, Dawn is a liability. I will not tell her about the negotiations. She is so unstable that she might talk. I can only tell her to trust me and all will be well. This morning, I telephoned the infirmary in Pozzuoli and talked to the doctor who looked after her at Davy's birth. We agreed she should go there as soon as possible.

I have just had good news. Braggiotti has been released. He telephoned me at noon and we spoke openly. He was put in a cage with every market professional in Milan. They quarrelled like cats. But he has seen Giuseppe and confirms that he is on the way to Zürich with the two telexes. I was right not to wait for Braggiotti. The Banca Commerciale is standing guarantor for his bail; but he is obliged to report to the Questura in Milan twice a day.

He is gloomy even beyond his wont. He says the market has been suspended until after Christmas for want of anybody to operate in it. This has not happened since the war. I laughed when he said this and he spoke sharply to me. There is no chance of the foreign institutions returning as buyers, he says. When trading is resumed on 27 December, they will be selling and washing their hands of the Milan casino for ever. The market will fall by as much as 25 percent. Not only Lamberti will be left with collapsing share values as collateral for his borrowings. Braggiotti named two smaller brokers. He says they will be selling to raise cash before the collateral is worthless.

It is time to move from my defensive position. It is time to buy, at last. I have told Braggiotti to go into the market an hour after opening tomorrow and buy every large-capi-talisation stock on the board. He is to go on buying until the market hits bottom. Cash will be deposited with him before the end of the year.

TEN

by William Nelson

It is 22 December today. I have not seen Chadwick for a week although I sometimes hear him, shouting for Dawn from somewhere in his apartments or talking to himself above me, while I sit in the sunshine by the almond tree beneath his window.

As the weather has brightened, Dawn has thrived, like a racehorse in spring. I do not know what happened while I was walking with Oriana, or what Chadwick said or did to Dawn. She seemed deranged with horror. I thought it would take weeks, months, for her to come right. Yet she slept that night and the next day, and it was as if nothing had happened. The burn on her right hand has healed and she carries no other signs of violence.

She woke me the next morning. She moved around the house with Amina, cleaning. Once I found her singing in the laundry. When I asked if perhaps I should leave, perhaps go to Oriana's in Capri so as to be at hand but not under her feet, she looked at me and said: No, why, unless you want to. I thought you were staying for Christmas. You can keep Jakob company. He likes you.

We have not spoken of what happened. Only in the morning, when she comes in and stands, carefully, just in the frame of the doorway, I ask if there is news and she shakes her head; and then tosses it up again and smiles and says: Buck up, Amina's put your coffee on.

She is closed up. She will not eat with us at Nella's or in the evening, and seems to touch nothing but her strange sandwiches of bread and chocolate. Nor will she paint. The tower room has not been touched. The toys remain on the tattered carpet, the canvas in place on the easel, the brushes

84

and paints on the sill. I asked her why she did not go on with the picture. She said she would wait, until Davy was back, and she needed rain for the light.

Chadwick scarcely exists for us. It is as if he exhausted his strength, or his shallow sense of duty, that first evening and Dawn must carry the burden. Perhaps grief and guilt are quantities to be passed between husband and wife. She has consolidated, while he has crumbled. From my place under the almond tree, I have heard him reciting something, softly and rhythmically as if it is verse. At other times, I hear her reading him the stock prices from *Il Sole* in a sort of sing-song as I read them six years ago, to the querulous, sick old man.

It may be the sunshine, but I keep recovering scraps from my earlier visit. *'Fiat, sei mila settecento, meno trecento, rendimento sei percento'*. I remember how the old man used to sit quietly, a blanket over his knees and his eyes closed, so that I sometimes thought he was sleeping; but if I missed a price, or made a mistake in translating the figures into words, he would open his eyes and ask me gently to repeat it.

In 1978, if we spoke of the old man, it was only in terms of his wants: the Saturday *Financial Times* or his bath or his whisky or the cigars that came from Davidoff in Geneva and were my reward for reading. Now, if Dawn speaks of Chadwick, it is to say that he is busy, or tired, or on the telephone and can I do something that he generally does: can I pick up the newspapers or walk the dog or help Amina with the provisions?

Where before I resented the distraction, I now enjoy it. I like walking out in the cool sunshine, carrying a bag with Bot, the terrier, pulling and Dawn still shouting last instructions, along the drive and down the shallow hill to Bocca d'Oro. I stand in the square under the planes, the pansies already out in the tubs, till the Christmas firecrackers send me away. I meet Giuseppe, standing by his yellow taxi, or the *marchese* in his transparent mackintosh, or Hoffmann being shaved by the deaf-mute barber, or Olgiata lounging by the bus stop. I feel at home. The newsagent, the pharmacist, the grocer stand up as I come in, put their heads on one side, and say: What news, professor, and I shake my head and they suck their teeth.

I have fallen into a routine, I buy what I am to buy and then join Hoffmann in the barber's shop and have myself shaved while he makes his telephone calls. His son is managing the saleroom in Zürich and, judging from Hoffmann's manner, needs unremitting advice. I lie back in the barber's chair, my face stinging from the cheap soap, and I am free of choice and responsibility for fifteen minutes. When the barber has finished, and I stand up, Hoffmann is always sitting quite still, as if listening. We walk, sometimes arm in arm, to Nella's and eat our delicious lunch. The lady can now even find fish for us. The marquis has taken to joining us: to smoke a cigarette, as he says, though he can be pressed to *grappa*. He may be too proud to take our hospitality for lunch and Hoffmann glared at me the only time I suggested it. Hoffmann orders his bottle of *grappa* and begins to ask questions.

At first, I did not realise he was questioning me. There seemed no method in it. He would be talking, about his childhood or the camp, or old Durward, or dealing with collectors and museums and suddenly I would find myself transported to the day of Davy's disappearance, Hoffmann staring at me through his small, watery eyes. At first, it infuriated me.

'For God's sake, Jakob, I had nothing to do with Davy's abduction. You know that. What motive could I have?'

'Ach, motives. Don't talk to me of motives.'

'Motive, motive,' said Crespi quietly. 'How can the motives of madmen be comprehended by the sane? My dear friend Dr Hoffmann knows this better than all men.'

'I'm not going to sit here to listen to this rubbish.'

'Now, now, William, you do not have to go. Sit down, please, I know you had no part in the burglary.'

'No I bloody well didn't.'

'How do you know that, Dr Hoffmann? Perhaps Mr Nelson has only skilfully covered his tracks.'

'I do know. Perhaps we should not tease the boy.' He

leaned forward so I smelled his breath. 'You remember I told Mrs Chadwick that I thought this was no common gang from Napoli or Calabria, but professional men? I was not quite honest. When my friend Durward died, I drew up for Dawn a list of the objects in the house. I did not want her inheritance to suffer from theft or mismanagement. My list included the two objects that are missing.'

He took a long drink of water. 'I knew the pieces well. First-quality work. Geoffrey bought them from my first saleroom in Zürich in 1955. I have spoken to my son by telephone and he has examined the sale catalogue. We had no photographs in those days, but he is sure. Neither the picture nor the silver barrel has a provenance.'

'Aha,' Crespi said. 'They are crude forgeries like my precious Ribera.'

'No, no. I have never sold forgeries. Unfortunately, I have, in the past, at the beginning of my business life, handled objects of doubtful provenance.'

'You mean, my dear Dr Hoffmann, that they were stolen in the first place.'

Hoffmann nodded his shaggy head.

'And were these,' I asked, 'the only objects in the house of doubtful provenance, as it were?'

Hoffmann nodded. He turned on me. 'You must understand the situation after the war, William. Europe was full of objects, and people, of doubtful provenance. Things without history, people without memory. Do not judge me harshly.'

'I wouldn't dream of it. But what does this mean?'

'This means that the thieves could place the objects in a sale, even at Christie's with the Press and pictures in the catalogue, and nobody would know they were stolen goods. I insured them myself in Zürich and they did not ask for photographs.'

'Jesus! Who knew that?'

Hoffmann looked down at his beautiful fingers. 'I and now you and the Marquis Franco.'

'And Signora Chadwick, no doubt,' Crespi said.

'And John Chadwick. Most important of all.'

'Why do you say him?' Hoffmann looked at me carefully.

'Oh for God's sake. You can see he's not sane. The child was terrified of him. You saw that, Franco, at the lunch. He stays all day in his room, talking to himself, I've heard him, while Dawn and I have to do everything to keep the place going. Now look what he has done. It beggars the imagination. To stage a burglary in his own house. Talk about working your assets. He raises insurance money on the picture and the wine cooler and then sells them discreetly, and separately, later on. Only he made a mistake. The men he used were after bigger returns and he's lost his only son. Can't you see, Jakob, that he's implicated? That's why he's not doing anything to find Davy.'

'You are jumping to conclusions, William. This is unwise.'

'I may be, but the circumstantial evidence is overwhelming. Franco, you heard what Braggiotti said. There's a mother and a father of a bear market in Italian stocks. He is probably heavily invested in Milan, if I know him. He's ruined.'

'He may be, William. But not Mrs Chadwick or little Davy,' said Hoffmann.

'How on earth would we know?'

Hoffmann laughed loudly. 'Let me tell you an old and bad Jewish story from before the war.' He put on an exaggerated storyteller's face, old and sly. 'It is about little Moritz, a Jewish boy in Germany. He is in the school and they are learning Roman history, the story about the gooses and the Capitol. And the Nazi teacher barks, 'What does our Jew know of the Capitol?' And Moritz, who is sleeping as always, wakes up and says, 'Herr Teacher, father told me I should not say. However, I understand our capitol is in the Credit-anstalt.' He looked at us in triumph. I laughed. Crespi nodded and smiled. 'It is a bad joke,' said Hoffmann. 'But Mrs Chadwick's capitol is in Switzerland. And I am trustee. When I saw Mr Chadwick, the first time, in Paradeplatz, I thought I will not trust him. *Es fehlt ihm Tiefgang.* I do not know that in English.'

'He lacks bottom. A graphic, if uncharitable phrase,' said Crespi.

'Look,' I said impatiently. 'He might have borrowed against her Swiss portfolio. You don't know that, Jakob. And he has sold her things. You can see from the marks on the walls that long-standing pictures have been sold. I know him, Jakob. He is a stock-market investor. It's the only thing he knows how to do. You must speak to him. It's our only chance of retrieving Davy.'

'He will not speak to me. It is useless. He will lie to me, just like my old friend Geoffrey Durward, who was also a stock-market investor. I can only listen to you.' His voice dropped suddenly and he murmured, 'And I can listen to Giovanni. And most important, to Davy.'

He was becoming sentimental. Crespi stirred uneasily.

Hoffmann sighed again. 'Let me explain. We cannot find Giovanni, the mad one. Why can we not find Giovanni, though there is a warrant for him from the court? Because he has no memory, just like the things that were stolen.'

'Of course,' said Crespi with irritation. 'Only memory creates or derives a pattern out of existence.'

'What about Davy? He has no memory, either.'

'*Oh doch*, William. Davy has a memory.' Hoffmann looked down at the table and began to speak so softly that both Crespi and I had to lean down to hear him.

'It must have been 1944 and winter, because the streets were full of mud. The transports were leaving again, every two or three days. All the others had gone already, except me and my brother Ariel. Then a transport arrived. Full. Five thousand children from Bialystok, to exchange with the English for war prisoners. I saw it on the cars: *Erholung und Austausch*. They were so sick and sad, we never saw such children. They would not go into the delousing, they were frightened from before, they were shouting, "Gas", so I jumped up and said we would take them in. Ariel and I took two boys by the hand to show them it was safe and then the others came, like sheep. We were mixed up with them and put in the family barracks and there was a heater and 500 grammes of bread extra every day. I took my best watch, an emerald Cartier, to the council of elders and we changed our place of origin: from Prague to Bialystok.'

'I was in the printing works when my man came from the council of elders. I hid in a box of paper for two days. When I came out, all the Polish children had gone. On 20 December, in the night. Some people said Lodz. I became a Danish boy. So I could search. I thought Ariel might have hidden, when they came for him. I went round our old places, his cobbler's booth, the bakery, the place where my father had taught Bohemian children, the barracks of the *Prominenten*, the café, the rose garden, the officers' casino were we sold watches for chocolate powder and bread. I thought myself Arik. I made myself Arik so I could find him. I walked with my hands along the wet walls of the barracks, hoping to touch a place where his hand had been already. This time I shall find him.'

He looked up. He was crying. He pulled out a large, bright handkerchief and dabbed his eyes without embarrassment. He drank some water which seemed to pass right through him and emerge as tears. Signora Nella hovered over us. Crespi put his hand on Hoffmann's and I felt, with a start, the helplessness of these two old men.

'So. Where shall we walk today?'

'To the haunts of the grave-digger,' said Crespi with drama.

We began at the cemetery. We examined a dirty grave. In the fresh earth, pansies were embedded by their stalks. I thought they must have been picked from the tubs in the square: pathetic evidence of Giovanni's piety. We talked to the priest, who made even Hoffmann impatient. He affected to have forgiven Chadwick for making the unauthorised burial and said he had dropped his law suit; but he spoke of sacrilege, and then of Davy's abduction, as if one followed the other with all the certainty of retribution.

We returned to the village and stood outside Giovanni's sealed house. The mourning poster was in tatters. We stared at the house for a while and then returned to the villa.

Each day that passes, as Christmas approaches, I drink my *grappa* and Hoffmann takes a last, reluctant gulp from his water glass. He says: Shall we do your walk again, let us get the marquis, and we extract Crespi from behind his useless stock and set off to the villa gate, where we turn and walk down towards the lighthouse. At the turning, I halt and Crespi walks on, swaying in an exaggerated manner and gesturing at some invisible companion, and I say to Hoffmann, here, just here, I stopped, while hunters' guns echo against the cliff and partridges burst out of the heather.

'And why did you not go to the Tiberio?'

He asks this every time and I reply every time, 'Because it was claustrophobic. There were hunters, like today. I told you I do not like gunfire.'

'And what about the Marchesa Oriana?' he asks.

'She wanted to join her father. I went to the village and drank a *grappa*. Ask the barman at the Scaline.'

Then we walk back down, in silence, up the road and Giuseppe is there with his car, waiting until Crespi returns from the bottom.

I try to think of Davy all the time, to see the world from his elevation, to peer up over the postcards at Crespi reading with horn-rimmed spectacles, to push with all my strength on the base of the barber-shop door. I stand at the bus stop and climb with difficulty up the steps of the Naples bus, before getting down again. But memories keep supervening from my last visit: my face in the barber's mirror as he shaved off a week's beard, the smell of the hot bus on the way to the lighthouse where Dawn bathed. I walk the streets with my eyes half-shut, conjuring a small figure, concentrating on his tiny steps, his big coat billowing out behind him. I stoop to touch garden walls and tree trunks, thinking to put my hand where he has put his. Once I dreamed I saw him in the attic, still wearing his mackintosh and drum, the roof dripping around him.

Another time—it must have been the 19th—I took them both up to the Tiberio, to show them the place which Davy liked, and Giuseppe and I pulled so hard on the rusty gate that the padlock cracked in two and we entered. Crespi knew the place well. He took us through the rye-grass and brambles to a summer house his father had built, with wrought-iron columns supporting a green copper roof, like a Turkish kiosk. Around us, the ground was uneven, as if it covered paths or broken cisterns or fallen columns. Crespi looked up to the sky and recited something in Latin, while gunfire boomed on every side.

I remembered whole pieces of my earlier visits to the garden: lying on the rye-grass with specimens of wild flowers resting on the dappled pages of Polunin, or the smell of French lavender, or the sight of the sea beneath the low wall at the end. On the way down, Hoffman looked so pale that I feared for him. When we returned to the house, just before sundown, Hoffmann stopped and looked at the back door, under the grand staircase, and the door to the hall at the top and said, 'So you left the back door open so that you could come back, without disturbing anybody, with the *marchesa.*'

I said, 'No, Jakob. That is not so. Chadwick wants you to think that.'

He nodded and said, 'Back door or hall door. Back door or hall door. Or perhaps another way in. Or no way in at all.'

Hoffmann left yesterday. He said he had business at home in Zürich, and Giuseppe took him to the Milan flight. Dawn and I were left alone, to run the house and minister to Chadwick, while a cold sun shone all day and all evening firecrackers burst in the street outside.

We bought and wrapped Christmas presents. I feared this would precipitate a crisis, but Dawn gave no sign of distress. She had been buying things for Davy all year and, after doing up her husband's calculator and Crespi's whisky and something interestingly shaped for me, we started on the toys. We set up a crib in the library. The figures, she said, were south German and had been bought by Hoffmann at one of his own sales for her fifth birthday. They were beautifully carved and quite untouched by worm. I collected straw for the stable floor and roof.

When we finished, Dawn stood up and said brightly: What a pity the Italians don't celebrate Christmas in a sentimental way, like the English and the Germans. Why don't we invite everybody to Christmas dinner? Giuseppe can kill one of his geese.

I rounded up what she called the usual suspects: Crespi, and through him his daughter, who is now in New York; the Giuseppes and Aminas, even Hoffmann, who is expected back. She told me not to invite Braggiotti. In one of those arbitrary swoops that occur every now and then in Italy, the entire Milanese stockbroking fraternity were taken from their homes by the financial police. All but Lamberti were released today; but Braggiotti is evidently not prepared to leave his practice untended, even on Christmas Day. We have asked Captain Olgiata and his wife instead.

Dawn's peace of mind troubles me, I no longer skirt the subject of Davy for she seems to enjoy talking about him: of the charms of a growing child, unique and yet banal, his titanic struggles with his surroundings, his fears and secrets. As we sit over lunch in the kitchen, she with her chocolate sandwiches and I with pasta and the red wine, she sometimes bursts out in laughter in the midst of talking of the boy. Then she reaches out and takes a cigarette, holding it like a paintbrush between the thumb and forefinger of her left hand; or we hear a shout from upstairs, beyond the library, and she gets up with *Il Sole* and I wander out with the wine to my place beneath the almond tree.

I have tried to tell her of my suspicion of Chadwick. I want to shake her complacency or pose till the truth falls out. But she shakes her head or gets up to do something else. I cannot comprehend her. How can her loyalty to her husband exceed her loyalty to her son? Here I am, sitting in clean, new sunshine, filling up my second exercise book, and I do not understand her.

We met in De Vere Gardens some time in the summer of 1976, I had just returned from Lebanon, in disgrace. The bank has never forgiven me for paying $100,000 in protection money to the local militias when I attempted to transfer the contents of the safe deposits from Bab Idriss. That year the auditors would not sign the bank's accounts, the stock price fell ten percent and the financial press in New York made hay. I was consigned to little trade financings that never even approached consummation. My old friends were doing other things, though I had once thought of us as a group, a generation tackling obstacles together like young hurdlers at Cheltenham. How the field had thinned, the course now strewn with blown or riderless horses! Those friends that had not died, or gone batty or lived abroad were absorbed in their work or their families. Dinner at their houses was torture. Conversation that had once been intoxicating now evaporated into different sorts of shop, of babies, or the markets, or newspapers and publishing houses. Chadwick himself was worst of all. He was the embodiment of stock-brokers' self-esteem.

That day, I was walking up to Kensington High Street, perhaps to buy cigarettes. It must have been high summer, for the sight of the sunlit cars driving west in a stream filled me with melancholy and pleasure. Perhaps I was hungover, for I drank a lot in those days.

I was certainly looking at the ground, for the first thing I saw was a pair of pink shoes; then ankles, bare legs, a flowered print dress and a large plastic carrier bag, which was falling; and cigarettes, jaffa cakes, eggs, tampons and potatoes, and other things wrapped in paper and plastic, falling.

The girl stood still. Her face, when I looked up at it, was frozen by the intrusion. Eggs had smashed at her feet and three oranges were rolling down towards the Albert Hall. I turned away from her and ran down, stopped the leading orange with my foot, and walked back towards her, picking up things as I came.

She had not moved, I think the light was shining through her dress and I could see the outline of her legs. I am sure she did not look like any girl I had seen before. Perhaps it was her ankles, which were a bit large, or the light through the print dress that made her seem vulnerable. The shock of the collision reverberated in my chest and the discovery of

94

her shopping was curiously intimate. When I carried the things to her flat, which was in Prince of Wales Terrace, I saw her easel and paints and felt I knew all there was to know.

We were neighbours. It would have been natural to spend time together; but my years in Beirut had broken my old circle and she seemed to know or want to know nobody. In those days, she was learning to draw at the Slade but I doubt if she was learning much. When she at last showed me her work, I forgot the all-purpose comments that I had prepared and just looked through the canvases, one by one. I tried to buy one, for they were very small, but she laughed and said she needed them for acres of wall in Italy.

I tried to kiss her, I had become mechanical with women, and nervous, and probably thought it insulting or unmanly not to seek to kiss a girl whom I liked. She pushed me away and said nothing for some time, looking at me with her small eyes. I realised she was angry and hurt. I apologised, I was relieved.

Our friendship had romantic undertones. How could that not be, when a young man and young woman spend their evenings together? But it was an alliance merely against individual solitude. She was uninterested in money or the City, she hated racing, tried but could not understand the Middle East and seemed to have no ambition of success in her profession. I realise now that her company was defensive for me, even snobbish: it was her strangeness and the individuality of her upbringing that attracted me. She allowed me to despise friends and activities that I could not utterly have foregone on my own.

In September, I was sent to Istanbul. I inherited an apartment at Emircan, overlooking the Bosphorus at its narrowest point. I longed to have her to stay and sit with me, drinking her beer in the evening and watching the Soviet shipping till night fell and the sea, for a moment, turned blue as ink. She did not come; her father was ill, and her Slade holidays, and then the term, she spent in Italy. I resolved to visit her, but received no encouragement; her letters, which were long and stuffed with every domestic detail in no order of importance, seemed self-contained.

Turkey became unsafe. The government changed as frequently as in Italy. The generals began to talk politics. A security expert from the bank's headquarters replaced the windows of my apartment and installed a remote-controlled lock on the garage, which I could never work. For a week, I took a different route to Taksim every day but then my old driver tired of it and we went back to the main road along the shore. On 10 April 1978, I travelled to Ankara for a meeting, about a new exchange control bill, with a minor official at the Finance Ministry. I met Paul Taylor of Citibank at the ministry and we caught the evening flight back together.

We were seated in the first-class section. As we drank our whisky, and talked business—Paul had no other conversation—we were not aware what was happening. Only when the woman across the aisle began to cry did I look up. There was a young man standing quietly at the entrance to the cockpit and carrying an automatic rifle with a hollow stock.

They were two: a big bully of a fellow, with a nervous, high-pitched shriek, and the silent young man. We thought they were Palestinians but they spoke Turkish to the cabin crew and another language I could not recognise (Kurdish, I learned later). The blinds were ordered drawn. Twice, we stopped for a while somewhere (though I did not know it, Beirut, first, and then Algiers). The ventilation was turned off and we sweated. Nobody was allowed to leave his seat. The place began to stink until I ceased to notice, Paul burst into tears when he could hold himself no longer; I had long since given in. The woman across the aisle wept without ceasing. The young man stood at the entrance to the cockpit, with one eye on the pilot and the other on us. He drank Pepsi-Cola constantly but never spoke or returned our smiles.

Paul was taken away first. We were halted at Ankara again, but I did not know this. We shook hands and then he walked down the aisle unaided, dignified in his stained suit, while

96

the fat man shouted at him. I listened but heard nothing. We took off immediately afterwards. I asked for cigarettes and was refused. I wept for much of the time and prayed for my life.

When I heard the wheels go down, I was sick. The young man gave me a paper bag, I heard a sound of movement behind me and I was sick again. All the passengers were coming forward, led by a big unshaven man in a badly fitting suit and a cloth cap. The boy did not even lift his gun. He began to urinate. Two men picked him up, as easily as if he were a cushion, and snapped his neck. They put him down in Paul's seat and shook me by the hand, the big man first and then one by one.

We were in Istanbul. I spent the night in hospital and, early in the morning, walked down to Sirkeci station. There was a train to Munich, I bought cigarettes and boarded it. I did not eat or sleep or shave. I could not sit still. I smoked. At Ljubljana, I got out and took a train to Trieste. At Trieste, there was a train to Venice. At Venice, I waited on the station for half a night and then took the express to Rome. At Rome station, I telephoned Dawn.

I do not remember how I got to the villa. I do remember sitting in the kitchen, with my arms resting on the table. Dawn was ironing socks. Amina was cooking something. I was on the point of saying something about Paul when I realised I felt tired and was hungry and wanted to shave my beard. I spent two days in bed until Dawn got me up to read to her father. It was my first taste of her routine.

I saw her only once more that year, when she came over for her exams. I invited her to the flat, I think after the races, but she was working hard and did not stay long. Later in the month, she married Chadwick at a grisly house in Bournemouth and they went back to Italy.

I was returned to doing export credits for insolvent countries. My memory became erratic. Just after the New Year, I began to suffer from insomnia. For two weeks, I did not sleep at all though I lay down in bed every night. I thought I would die of my company every minute and second without relief.

I gave up alcohol and took sleeping pills for six months till I collected some scraps of will and threw the bottle and prescription into a skip on the Gloucester Road.

I did not visit the Chadwicks. In the daytime I despised myself for resenting Dawn, though in the hours of the night, self-pity engulfed me. I knew very well that I had treated her for my own convenience. Even as I walked down through the smog to Sirkeci or stood on the platform at Ljubljana, I must have been thinking of her as a support: a friend from childhood, perhaps, or a sister. At the villa, I submitted to her fagging and the oddities of the house, for I had no equivalent structure for my own life. I could offer her nothing, because my self-respect was ruined. She realised this and chose Chadwick, as if from a hat, and I had affairs with women I came on by accident, who were affectionate and easily hurt. On Saturdays I walked around Kensington, too weary to buy anything in the shops. On Sundays I sat in strange churches, thinking thoughts that resembled prayers. I travelled a lot. I paced up and down airports, bursting with guilt or desire, or lay on hard hotel beds in rooms littered with used bookmatches. In 1983, an article on Aids in the *Spiegel* brought a return of my insomnia. I began playing with the idea of suicide, not seriously, but as a course of action not necessarily to be excluded.

I knew I was falling to bits. I woke up anxious and went to bed anxious and anxiety accompanied me through the day. Quite soon, I would forget how I had been: curious, moderately intelligent, quite daring. I knew I must try and follow the thread back through the last six years and find the places where I had gone wrong. I knew I must see Dawn, and the Villa Crespi, again.

In the past ten days, the house has become familiar. I remember my first visit and see no differences but samenesses. The name of the house male has changed but not his habits. Chadwick is not responsible for this madhouse. I was misled by my jealousy of him. Chadwick is simply a new part in a mechanism that was in place six years ago. The mechanism functions, but so inefficiently that it consumes every moment of the day in its service, leaving no time for restlessness or regret. Questions are not asked nor answered. Conversation dies away. Mealtimes, with their succession of small courses to be brought and served, pass in silence or are shouting-matches. This is not Chadwick's world.

It is Dawn's world. I know from her painting that this ugly house, with its muddle of old things, some broken, all dirty, is bursting with meaning for her. She looks on the house and its objects with a child's intensity of interest. It is her picture of childhood.

In a moment, she will call. It is time for me to take Bot up to the Tiberio. I am part of her world. I drink too much, and sit quietly under the almond tree while she is reading to Chadwick. I take Bot for a walk when she has finished. I am as shy, spoilt and lazy as Chadwick.

Poor John Chadwick. He was made to be a City clerk. He never deserved this life. No wonder he hits her every now and then. No wonder he chips away at her inheritance. No wonder....

It is the afternoon of 22 December. The tangle is unrav-elling. John Chadwick has stolen the two objects. Even Hoffmann and Olgiata must know that. I think he arranged Davy's disappearance.

It is now fairly simple. I am sure Davy is nearby and safe. It is a matter of arranging the pictures I have: the grave tended by Giovanni, the tattered mourning-poster, Giovanni in the tower with the drum. I see Davy indoors, warm, laughing and clapping his hands as Giovanni beats my red drum.

It is time to walk quietly along the wall of the house and run into the pines.

ELEVEN

by Dawn Chadwick

Darling Davy, I am writing a long time ago. If you have this letter and all the other papers, it means that Herr Hoffmann thinks it is time. His father was our great friend and helped find you that Christmas you went away and I was at my wits' end and did not know what happened or if you would ever come back. Work hard, even when the work seems boring and you are homesick, for it is a good job and you will always be able to work even when other people can't. Herr Hoffmann's father, the old man, said it saved his life in the war. People will always need watches and will need to have them mended when they break. I am doing what I think is right for you, as I have always done. You must believe that, Davy.

It is a lovely day. The winter was so horrible, with you having whooping-cough, and the roof leaking. I thought it would never end but it has now. When I walked this morning down towards the lighthouse, all the rosemary was out and it smelt so delicious. I am sitting in my bedroom, on the bed, and I can hear you outside, playing with old Bot, who is getting cross. Oriana has just been, on her way back to Capri, looking so smart I was envious, and we stared out through the bars at you both. I know I should go out, too, because I have just seen Giovanni skulking in the garden and he always digs everything up unless it is actually attached and I do not want him near my new tulips which cost a fortune and came from van Tubergren.

But if I do not write this now, I never will. There is always so much to do, what with the house and the garden and Oriana driving up in her swanky car. One of these days, she is going to pull out a lot of money and say can she have the

100

villa back and then I won't have any friends. Or perhaps, by the time Ariel gives you this letter, she will have moved in and we will be in the village and I will have a shop or do the police uniforms like Amina's mother used to do before she took to the bottle.

After you came back, I thought I should write everything down so you could read it, when you were a bit older, and understand. Your father said I would just muddle it up or make it seem that I behaved better than I actually behaved. But then Amina found the two blue exercise books which Willie Nelson left behind when he went and I was so cross at the things he said I thought I should have my own say.

Your father did not care about the exercise books at all. He says that everybody sees things differently and sometimes you cannot see that two people are describing the same event or conversation. I started reading the exercise books to him but he told me to stop after the first page because he wanted nothing to do with Willie again and that if Oriana came, that was my business. In fact, Oriana once asked to have them back and I lied to her, saying that we had never seen the books, we thought Willie had taken them when he went on Christmas Day. I haven't needed to tell many lies for you, Davy, but I told that one. She has never asked again.

The cassettes are your father's. I used to hear him at night, while you were away, speaking into the machine because he does not take notes. I found them stuffed into a bookcase in the library and I thought I would play them and write it all down so you could read what he was saying at the time. But your father said it was a waste of time and told me to throw them away and I could not work the player and so I will put them in together with the player, which you can mend, or you jolly well should be able to mend. Jakob used to say you had better fingers than he had, but he was such a flatterer, Davy, when it suited him.

There should be five cassettes. I don't know if they are in any special order but I don't think it matters. If you have read this far, perhaps you should stop and listen to the tapes

101

and read Willie's two books first. I am not a good writer like Willie and I don't understand all the money side of it like your father. I can just tell you what happened and it's not at all like what Willie says or, probably for that matter, what your father says. I did something wrong, Davy, and you must know about it.

It is hard to know where to begin the story. I cannot begin with the day you went away, because things that had happened long before played a part in your going. So I will begin with me. I was born in Sandy, Bedfordshire on your birthday in 1956. Your great-grandfather had a brickworks there. He had been a farmer, and had married a farmer's daughter who was so pretty that they put her face on the biscuit tin which you used to like in my bedroom. She died young and I am named after her.

Your great-grandfather knew everything there was to know about bricks. Your grandfather did not give a fig for them. But that is England for you. Whenever you have something really good, like a brickworks that you have built yourself, your heirs never want to work in it; or at least, my father didn't and nobody thought of asking my aunts.

That's why I did not mind you not going to school in England. I did not want you to be like your grandfather, who was at Eton, and John was anyway dead set against it. My father scarcely ever went to the works and I think the men minded that, though I used to go a lot even as a child. I loved seeing the clay cut by the new machine, like an enormous egg-slicer, and then feeling the hot blast from the tunnel as the bricks went in. I learned how to make bricks by hand and could do 250 an hour which was quite good. Sometimes I wish we had stayed in England and not sold the business so you could have run it.

My mother did not care for it either. She had grown up in Newmarket, because her father had trained Lord Derby's horses. She was rich; well, I suppose we were, too, in a way.

We moved to a bigger house near Bury St. Edmunds. The house smelt of gin, and the smell was so strong and raw I thought I would faint sometimes. There were sweets everywhere in little silver dishes. Many of the really good things, like the Tompion and the Georgian silver, came from that house. I suppose she brought them with her. My father also collected things all his life, but they were things that nobody thought precious at the time and he bought for nothing off Herr Hoffmann; like the small Dutch pictures or those watercolours of the Bay of Naples on dark paper or the Venetian blackamoors in the library or the Turkish watches,

Your grandfather became interested in racing and they spent a lot of time at Newmarket. They had a house in Jamaica, too, which is a ruin now because nobody dares live in it. I never went there. I do remember them quarrelling about something and screaming for them to stop because I could not understand how they could not agree on everything. She died when I was seven, cruising with her sister on a ship called the *Lakonia* which caught fire off the coast of Portugal. When they finally put the fire out and towed the ship to harbour, they could find no trace of either of them in their cabins. Sometimes I wonder if my mother might not suddenly arrive at the villa one day, big and blonde and smelling of gin in the way it used to smell.

I do not know when the Bury house was sold. It must have been before we went to live abroad, I think for tax. We spent a gorgeous summer in Zürich, or it might have been two, seeing old Herr Hoffmann and his young son (who was very quiet and good-looking and never did anything wrong). Old Herr Hoffmann was my father's great friend. He had been in a terrible concentration camp in Czechoslovakia and lost his family, including his brother, who he always talked about and was also called Ariel, I think. Your grandfather, who was in intelligence, helped him escape from the Russian part of Vienna just after the end of the war.

Your grandfather was always terribly rude to old Herr Hoffmann, called him a thieving Jew and that sort of thing and used to say he had only saved him in Vienna because he was carrying valuable watches he had stolen from the poor people in the camp. In fact, he loved him very much and we used to go everywhere together, to Vienna and Salzburg and Munich and places like that. My father had a way of making me feel grown-up. He let me stay up late and wear make-up and order for myself in restaurants. But with Herr Hoffmann I could ride the trams and hide in the vintage cars in his auction room and eat chocolate all the time.

It must have been the year after Zürich that we moved to the villa. I was very sorry when my father sold the brickworks, especially to London Brick, which makes those awful flettons they have on the back walls of cinemas in England. It was also during a slump, which happens every five years in bricks come wind or shine because people always make too many and the price falls, so we did not get as much money for it as my father hoped.

But even then the villa cost half a million lire a month to keep up, a lot of money in those days, and my father was still interested in horses. We had quite a good one, a colt called Don Ascanio, who won a good race at the Cascine in Florence and we were going to breed from him but it never came to anything. Your grandfather was a dreamer, you see. There was a sort of myth that somehow the horses paid for themselves and one of them would come right one day, which of course never happened. But my father sold them in about 1970, I think because old Herr Hoffmann made him. What was worse was that he also had a girlfriend in the village, though she is dead now and I did not find out about it until Herr Hoffmann showed me the will. I was terribly upset because he did not tell me about her or about Giuseppe, who is really my younger brother and your uncle, and I never told anybody else, not even your father.

I loved the villa. People used to say that it was too dark and cluttered and there were no straight lines so none of the furniture fitted but if you grow up in a house, as you and I have done, you get to know every inch of it and you cannot imagine living anywhere else. Even then, we did not see many people; only Franco, who sold us the house (which took seven years to go through), and the people who worked here like Amina and her family. My father used to quarrel with everybody over silly things, with Franco because he was going on about his family or even with Jakob. He would stalk around shouting: I'm not having anything to do with the filthy Jew, I'm not having him my executor and so on. But they all made it up, somehow or other, and he never changed his will, although he once called the *notaio* to come all the way from Pozzuoli.

I am one of those people who likes looking after a house, cleaning and ironing and everything. A natural drudge, your grandfather used to call me but I didn't mind. I used to feel so proud, walking out with him, arm in arm, to Nella's or to Franco's shop in the village. He used to smoke enormous cigars like Sir Winston and everybody treated him like a grandee. I felt there was so much in Bocca d'Oro that I would never need to go anywhere else, not even Zürich, though we went there every year to sell things. What money we got probably ended up as hay for the Don or tat for poor Giovanna in the village.

I don't suppose I learned much. Your grandfather used to say I was completely uneducated and a good thing, too, though I had learned all those languages, French and German and Italian, when I was a child and we were travelling. I went to the *asilo*, just like you only in those days it was at the other end of the village by the gravel pit, and then with Oriana to a school run by a very snobbish lady at Caserta. But since I did not board, and it took so long to get there and back by taxi, we gave it up after only two terms and that is why your old mother is such a fool.

My father said he would teach me. I read an awful lot; all of Waverley by the age of twelve and things nobody reads any more, like Tasso and Spenser. What I enjoyed most, of course, was drawing. I won the prize for drawing at Caserta and Herr Hoffmann said I was talented and should go to Munich to study. In the end, I did a picture for the Slade and was accepted there instead.

When I told your grandfather, he just laughed and laughed.

I did not particularly want to go, but I was twenty which is an obstinate age as you will see. I was curious about England. I wanted to see if I really could paint, which was the only thing I had of my own. And I suppose I wanted to go out a bit. The only young men I knew were the awful Pasquale, the priest's nephew, and Giuseppe and he was much younger. Thank God he was much younger, because he did not know we were brother and sister.

My father just laughed. He said Amina was a better cook and Pasquale was a better reader. I know he was hurt and brooded about it. I suppose he thought he was being abandoned again by women, as his mother and his wife had abandoned him. Perhaps he actually wanted me to go, because that is what he expected and then he could feel sorry for himself.

The silly thing is that I could not really enjoy London, thinking about the villa. I was always either guilty or defiant. The work was all right but I never went out. I did not have any money, anyway. I suppose I had become so Italian that London seemed a cold, dull place; and I kept finding fault with everything simply because I was in a temper. The only friend I made was Willie. I met him by accident in the street. He had grown up in Newmarket, too. We spent all our evenings together. I think it was an easy way of not staying at home.

I liked him so much then. He was nervous and sad, and he made such heavy weather of life, like a child growing up. In those days, he worked at First City Bank. He had just come back from Beirut, in disgrace, although it was not his fault. It was during the troubles there, or at least the first lot, and he was told to move the money from the bank vaults to a safer place. He had to bribe all the local gangsters to let the money out, but then other groups heard about it and when it came time to move the money, there was a big gunfight and shells and rockets and they had to go back into the vaults. So they lost all the protection money and the stuff had to stay in the vaults and was stolen a year later, after Willie had gone.

He was very resentful about it and hated everything, especially London, for he missed the Middle East, as I missed the villa. I suppose that is why we got on so well together. He used to talk about the Middle East a lot, knew all about the different types of Palestinians and if ever a bomb went off or someone was shot he always had a name for who had done it and what would happen next.

His other love was racing. He was just like my father. He had a useless old handicapper, called Lucky Lout, I think, who was always coming fourth at places like Ludlow and Towcester, but he talked about it as if it would one day win a Gran Premio. He was sentimental and always put a fortune on its back and did not mind when I refused to come with him, because he took it all very seriously. He had been a race-rider himself once, but I think he had too much imagination for it and let his weight go so he could not ride. He never got up on Lucky Lout, saying he was far too valuable for an amateur to ride.

I used to write to my father every day but he never wrote back, not even by dictation. When I went over the first summer, I found Pasquale well installed. He read in an affected voice and used to take my father's arm on his walk. He had lovely new suits. What made me really lose my temper was when my father gave him one of the watercolours of Naples. I can be quite strong, when I want to, Davy, and there were terrific rows. My father kept saying that he would get the *notaio* up, just to hurt me. In the end, I won. Pasquale was sent away, with a silver teapot, and good riddance. I was too proud to give up the Slade, but I only spent a bit of the term in London and none of the holidays. I worked at the villa and got to know Capodichino till I could scream.

Your grandfather was getting old so quickly. He could scarcely see at all to walk and we used to go only as far as the Scaline, drink a *ramazotti* and come back again. He became pale and lost weight. I think he was bored with life or just too lazy to go on with it and angry. But, Davy, I loved that horrid, spoiled old man so much, more than anybody else but you, my darling. Sometimes I felt so sorry for him that I

107

would creep into his bed at night and hug him, as you used to do with me.

At the beginning of 1978, my last year at the Slade, he gave up walking for good. It was bitter weather, with a *tramontana* and raining all the time, and we took him to the Carmelite sisters. Dr Carrai, who was the doctor who looked after me when you were born, said he could see no real deterioration. Your grandfather was still alert. You know, I think he enjoyed having me help him undress and go to the loo and everything, because he was angry. Mad old Giovanni was marvellous. You know he is so strong, that he could carry your grandfather down the stairs to his wheelchair. They only ever went to the cemetery. I suppose it was the only walk the poor fellow knew. I think my father liked to hear him chattering, although I don't suppose he listened.

In April, Willie came from Istanbul. He was in a terrific state. His aeroplane had been hijacked and his friend, another banker, was shot and thrown out on the runway. He had not eaten or slept for days and he stank. I had to let him stay, although my father was furious and refused even to refer to him by name except as Dawn's male guest or worse.

Willie was pathetic. He would stay up all night drinking whisky in the tiled hall upstairs. He did not eat, or read, or go out, or even talk much, because his memory was not working properly. Dr Carrai came and gave him some very strong sleeping pills but I took them away again, because I was worried about him.

Men are such fools, Davy. They go out, looking for adventure, and when they find it they don't like it and come scurrying back to a woman's skirts. He thought he had failed in some way and that he could never do anything else. You know what a fagger I am. I made him do all the jobs in the house till Giuseppe became jealous and got him to read the newspaper and memoirs to your grandfather, which I was no good at. He read well, without too much expression like Pasquale, not that my father thanked him.

There is nothing nicer than seeing somebody recover. Willie started sleeping. He cut down on his drinking and smoking and was able to talk about what happened. We spent a lot of time together. We used to have lunch outside the kitchen, or in Nella's, and he knew so much about the world and had been to so many places that he was good company. You know, Davy, I had met so few young men, not like Oriana, who was always turning up with different boys with perfect manners but nothing to say for themselves. I felt I had given all my life to my father and he had taken everything. Even my time at the Slade, which is supposed to be the best fun in one's life, he had spoiled.

Willie and I used to go for walks, to the lighthouse and to the garden on the cliff which you used to call your place. I felt guilty, of course, and perhaps I wanted to punish my father. But the spring flowers were even better than usual that year and I got out for Willie Polunin's book on Mediterranean flowers. He went mad for collecting specimens and writing notes in the margins of the book, which was absolutely forbidden but I did not tell him so.

I knew that an awful row would break as soon as he had left. But I kept putting it off. We used to spend whole afternoons up at the garden, sitting in that little kiosk that the Crespis built, or on the floor of the cistern, which was not as overgrown then. Because nobody went there but us, and there were no goats, it was a wonderful place for specimens and Willie would lay them out carefully on the pavement of the cistern and bury himself in Polunin while I used to draw or look at the rocks below. Willie had also discovered all those nasty passages about Tiberius in the Roman authors that make all the queers in Capri squeal, but I never found the place at all sinister. To me it was just the remains of a villa, with a big cistern to hold rainwater, for there is no spring up there. And lots of cistus.

But there wasn't a row when Willie left. Two days later, Amina went up to give your grandfather his bath and found him quite cold. She washed him all the same and he was buried that afternoon. The whole village came and Franco read a lesson and cried buckets.

I felt neither sad nor relieved but frightened. I felt as if the villa had fallen down, leaving me crashing about in the ruins. Old Herr Hoffmann came and we spent two days going over the house and my father's business affairs. They were a terrible mess. Quite apart from the Giuseppe business, your grandfather owed Braggiotti alone nearly a million lire for shares he had bought. Jakob said I should sell the house and come and live in Switzerland, perhaps at Ascona, but I could not do that, Davy. He took our best picture, the Salvator Rosa which is now in Pittsburg, and some other things to pay off the debts and give something to Giuseppe. I could not bear to stay in the house alone. I felt sick all the time and had nothing to do round the house. So I went back to England.

I don't know what I was looking for. I finished my picture for the Summer Exhibition and started going out. I saw Willie only once. I know he sort of liked me, Davy, but I couldn't bear it, I wanted nothing to do with that time at the villa, I wanted to start all anew with people who hadn't known your grandfather. Your father asked me to marry him just a week or two later and I was glad to say yes, for it gave me something to look forward to. His parents had retired to Bournemouth and we were married in a registry office there. I remember the seafront was full of couples. Willie got very plastered at the wedding and there was a dreadful scene when he made some patronising remark to John's mother.

We spent our honeymoon in Venice. It was not a great success. I am a hopeless traveller and the place is so mouldy. The alleys were always crowded and the restaurants cost a fortune. I hurt my foot in a church, which was a good thing because then we could not walk so much. Davy, the place gave me a sort of fever. On the lagoon, where we spent most of our time, I felt I was hanging between the air and the water, not knowing which smudge on the horizon was Torcello tower and which a fisherman on stilts. We were very shy of each other. In the restaurants, your father would talk of this picture or that picture we had seen, but they all seemed to merge in my memory and it did not seem to matter who had painted what. I'm sure Tintoretto was a syndicate.

Sometimes I felt so sick I did not want to get up.

In the end, your father agreed to come down to the villa. I was so relieved that I bribed the guard on the train to give us a sleeping compartment, which shocked your father horribly. I think he had not realised he had married an Italian.

TWELVE

by Dawn Chadwick

You were a dreadful child, Davy. That first winter I thought I was going to die. Nothing I could do would stop you crying. It's a terrible thing to say, but I understand why some mothers are driven to hitting their children. At times, I even got so far as lifting my hand until I remembered myself and stopped.

I did up the tower room for you and used to sleep there myself, rather than pad around the house every time I heard you. I hardly saw your father, and but for Amina, who sometimes took you to her own house, I really might have gone mad. I was tired all the time. I had no milk and when you got older, I became fat from eating all the things you wouldn't eat. Your father could not understand what was wrong, for he was building his library a long way from the tower, and looked hurt if his lunch was spoiled or, worse, as if he had made some awful mistake in marrying me.

I felt so hopeless. Amina only had to lift you up for you to stop crying and smile, in that way you still have. For almost a year, I hardly went outside and when I did, perhaps to weed, blinking in the sunshine, then you began again. I did not know what frightened you. I wondered if it were the house, and I had Giuseppe do up your room again in light colours and filled it with lamps but it did no good. I thought it might be something wrong with me and went back to the Carmelite sisters, but Dr Carrai told me to stop making such a fuss.

I felt so guilty, Davy. I wondered if I had done something wicked to be visited with such a monster and I used to go up to the church, when you were with Amina, and sit for hours not so much praying as talking to myself. I got the

112

batty idea that I should do confession, but the horrid *parroco* would not hear it unless I became a Catholic and I could not do that. Your grandfather would have turned in his grave.

I became morbid. I used to collect spring flowers from up by your place and place them on my father's grave till Franco told me I was becoming like Ophelia and I should pull myself together. He used to tease me by reading the most overdone bits of Swinburne or that dreadful scene from *The Bride of Lammermoor* when Lucy goes mad. Oriana came to stay and helped a lot although she kept bossing your father about and he became cross. Even she, who only really liked doing it rather than the consequences, could keep you quiet and make you eat.

Then you started to speak and it all became better. Of course, it had to be Amina that you spoke your first words to, and you knew far more Italian than English till you were nearly five. But it was as if, now you could speak, you could utter your frustrations. This was the happiest time in my life, Davy. It seemed as if the sun was always shining, I suppose because we went outside at last. Giuseppe and I made you a paddling pool with some good bricks we picked up when the old *asilo* was knocked down and I could spend the afternoon with the garden but keep my eye on you, playing there. We used the rest of the bricks to build a parapet on the edge of the hill so that you could not stray over. You became brown from the sun and your hair was like straw, all shiny and yellow.

I thought you might be lonely, later on when you got older, and I didn't mind about you being so difficult at the beginning, but your father said we couldn't really afford more children, and that was that. I swore to myself that I would devote all my life to you and your father and make the villa perfect. I became so proud of you that I wanted to show you off and we started having people up to the house, even from England. But your father usually managed to quarrel with them over something or the other and it was only the real stayers, like Franco or Dr Braggiotti, who ever came back.

Your godparents were marvellous in their different ways.

Oriana was always sending back glamorous little presents from New York or Paris or places like that. I remember a Dior sailor-suit which you wore to a party in the village and which shrunk to nothing in the wash. Old Herr Hoffmann usually had some sort of business with your father, but I think sometimes he came specially to see you. We had such plans for you, he and I. He said you would be a great craftsman and would be his apprentice, but I could not bear the thought of you going away even if I went to live at the Baur au Lac to be near you.

You loved Zürich, when we went there. The preparations took so long and were always so hectic but I felt so proud, standing on the station platform, with Giuseppe holding your hand and your father counting the luggage. Then at the Baur au Lac, you used to do what I loved doing as a child, running up and down the long passages and nobody seemed to mind until you ran into a chambermaid with her trolley and everything was upset.

Once, old Herr Hoffmann took us to Bayreuth. I suppose it was rather stupid, the Germans hating children and being such bores about Wagner, but when the man on the door said you could not come in and all the people sucked their teeth, Jakob just turned round and walked to the queue where the students were waiting without a chance of getting in and gave them our five tickets which had a cost a quarter of a million lire each.

As a consolation, we went to *Lucia* at San Carlo and you sat perfectly still all the time except when she came on—I think it was Mara Zampieri—and then you stood up and clapped your hands. I teased you that you had fallen in love with her and you got furious and ran round the room till I stopped. I wrote to her and she sent a signed photograph but it got lost.

I wondered sometimes if I had not invested too much in you, rather like your father who was always talking about a balanced portfolio. Sometimes I was so fearful for you, especially when the kidnappings were going on. I used to keep your father up at night worrying about it, and then an

English child was kidnapped in Sardinia and I could not sleep at all. I know that we were not rich, or at least not any more, but how was some Calabrian or *camorrista* to know that, and I made your father change the locks on the house and get a special burglar alarm from Germany.

I knew that if I ever lost you, all the sun would go from me, as it did that first year, and I would be fat and blind like a worm. I knew that I had rolled up the world till it looked like you. I did not care if we were rich or poor or popular or unpopular. I wouldn't have minded being ill if it had meant that you were well. And all the time, I knew that I was running a dreadful risk, that I was too happy for our own good and the world was a jealous place.

I do not know what you remember from that Christmas of 1984. You were very dirty when we found you, but you were cheerful. Dr Carrai examined you and was amazed that you hadn't even caught cold. You came back as you went away, wearing the same red mackintosh you had made so dirty in the cemetery that morning, as if you had simply slept for a fortnight; or as if all the clocks at Villa Crespi had stopped at six o'clock in the evening from 15 December to Christmas Day.

It was as cold a winter as the year you were born. It is the time of year I hate. The boys throw firecrackers in the street so that, by Christmas, you think you are in the middle of a battle. There is nothing for the people to do in the village and the men sit around playing billiards and shooting harmless birds and sleeping with one another's wives. That year, it blew a *tramontana* all the time and the storms were terrific. The swimming platform by the lighthouse was dashed away to sea and Amina's mother got drunk and lost her footing on the cliff by the Tiberio and was not found for a day. The priest said that she could only have gone up there to kill herself and would not let her be buried in the churchyard and Amina came to live with us because she didn't dare go out at night or to her home for fear of the spirit.

Every year, your father said he would get the roof properly seen to, but Giuseppe had that Italian passion for the makeshift. And every year the tiles blew off and the water came in like the Flood. Your father was preoccupied with other matters. I know now that his investments were not going well, just like your grandfather's at the end of his life, with that hellish stock market which is no better than a racecourse. I think that is why he invited Dr Braggiotti down to the villa on the day that you went away.

Willie was staying. He was as nervous and highly wrought as ever, but he was different from that first time. I know he hoped that the villa would once again rescue him from his nerves and gloom but he was less passive. He quarrelled with your father at once, for they were just like any other men, who cannot have friendship without rivalry, and I think he suspected about the investments. And, Davy, he still liked me and I made sure I had Oriana at my side so that she could work her magic as she always did. I sort of knew there was going to be trouble, but I could never have dreamed what kind of trouble.

For as long as I live, I shall never forget 15 December 1984. I woke to the rain and I went to the bed with the rain and at times I thought I would drown in the rain. When I went to wake you, it was already pouring into the attic. We ransacked the house for buckets and bowls and it still made a pool in the library and even leaked through the dining-room ceiling right onto the table where we were sitting.

We had prepared the lunch the day before. I felt so restless, so anxious, that I went to work on a picture I was doing, of your toys in the tower room. Willie joined me after a while, and then your father, who was in a terrible mood. Giovanni had come, speechless with excitement, and it was some time before your father could make any sense of him. Giovanni said he would not bury the old lady in the field behind the church, whatever Don Ambrosiano said, he would rather lose his job or put the body on the high altar until that cruel man relented.

Your father was very good at things like that. Your grandfather had bought a plot in the graveyard just before his death, when he spent all his time there with Giovanni, and there was room enough for everybody and to spare. The rain was bucketing down and nobody would see if Amina's mother was buried there. He had found an English prayer book and they set off, with you to divert attention, wrapped up against the rain and wind.

By the time you returned, we had all sat down to lunch: Franco Crespi, Oriana who was flirting shamelessly with Willie, and Dr Braggiotti who had arrived from the airport with Giuseppe. The church party was indescribably muddy, especially you, but also your father who refused to change. I suppose that he did this on purpose, so that nobody could settle down and enjoy a normal lunch party such as other people have, where they talk about sensible things. At his end of the table, he kept teasing poor Giovanni and Amina about how boozy the old lady was and how if they did not drink up, her spirit would come round and sip from their glasses. Giovanni, who is superstitious as well as everything else, got in a terrible stew.

But Franco is so mischievous. He knew that Braggiotti had not come down all the way from Milan just for a lunch and he knew your father was trying to keep off the subject of the stock market. He kept asking questions and your father was getting more and more upset till he stood up and started screaming at Franco that the Crespis were no good, that they were bankrupt and would soon be forgotten. Davy, I could not stand it, and nor could you. It was so unfair, because it wasn't Franco's fault that he had to sell the house to us and run a shop, it was his father's, and he was our greatest friend despite all the rudeness he had from my father and from your father.

I stood up and started shouting. And your father's eyes went black, as they used to do when he was really livid, when he was absolutely terrifying and the only thing to do was run from him. But it was you, Davy, who shut everybody up. I'd never seen you like that, or not since that awful first year. You scrambled up on the table, upsetting Oriana's glass. You were still wearing your dirty red mackintosh and your eyes were screwed tight shut and your knuckles pressed hard against the sides of your head and your face whiter than the table-cloth. And you were shrieking, 'Let me go. Let me go.'

I had to carry you up the stairs. You were just a dead weight, and your head lolled to the side. Your tongue was stuck between your lips which only used to happen when you were really unhappy. I put you in bed and tried to undress you but when I tried to get your mac off, you hit me so hard in the bosom that I left you as you were, with your mac and shoes on.

I sat with you for a while, listening to your breathing and Giovanni banging his buckets next door. I felt so depressed, Davy. It was not so much the lunch which was spoiled, though that was bad enough: why couldn't we have an ordinary lunch, for an honoured family friend from Milan, just like other people? It was much worse than that. I thought that one day you would just get up and say, I've had enough of this loony bin, and just walk out of the door and not come back.

In the end, I went down to my room. I had drunk too much and cried too much and felt old and fat and heavy. It was 4.15 by the Atmos clock on my dressing table, which old Herr Hoffmann gave me because he said it would keep the right time for 400 years and we could set the other clocks by it though we never did. Your father woke me at 7.05 and told me to come downstairs to the dining room. It was almost dark, and the lights didn't work because of the storm, though John had a torch.

In the light of the torch, I could see Amina had washed up. The only odd thing in the room were two dirty glasses on the gas fire. From the marks on one rim, I knew they were Giovanni's, because he always makes such a mess from that disgusting snuff he eats. I smiled because I thought that, after finishing with the buckets, he had needed some Dutch courage so he could face the unquiet spirit outside.

Something else was wrong. I looked round the room and saw that one of the pictures was missing and the walls were covered in brown stuff. I put my hand to it, Davy, and it was shit and I was sick, there all over the floor, till your father

118

carried me out to the kitchen sink.

I didn't know what was happening. Willie was there, still in his coat, and they were fighting and punching each other. I was thinking of you, Davy. All my thoughts were of you. I told Willie to go up and get you and take you to Signora Nella's. I did not want you to see what had happened, I was so frightened. Then I rang up old Herr Hoffmann, because he was the man who always helped us, and then Willie was back and the men were fighting again. I ran upstairs but I hit my shin against a step in the dark, and I was crying with pain when I came into your room.

I knew you had gone, even though it was dark. Even when you never made a sound, when you were hiding in the cupboard or behind Amina or under your bed, I always knew but I spun it out, saying: Now, where could he be, not here, not here, until you laughed and I'd pounce. I walked over to the bed. The sheet and blankets had been turned back neatly but where you had lain was cold.

I suppose I fainted because the next thing I remember was John shining a torch in my face and slapping me. He took me downstairs to my room and gave me two Quanyl. He kept saying: Don't worry, I've got it in hand, don't worry, Davy is all right, till he turned the torch off and I went out with it.

THIRTEEN

by Dawn Chadwick

I cannot describe what I suffered while you were away, Davy. I know this will sound mad but I was mad. I thought that you had gone of your own accord. I could imagine you so easily, walking down the drive in your mackintosh in the rain, down the path to the village and out, into places you didn't know, beyond the gravel pit towards Pozzuoli, or through the gardens towards the Faro.

Even when I saw Captain Olgiata and the man from the Generali, and they told me about the picture and the wine cooler, and we had cleaned up everything in the dining room, I still couldn't get the idea out of my mind. Only now I thought of men coming into the house while we were sleeping, and I knew the house would never be safe again and that men could break in when they wanted.

I could not think of you in their hands. I dared not go about the house, even with the lights on. And in the passages when the time-switch flicked off, I felt like screaming because I could not touch the wall or lean against a chair for fear of what was on it. I threw away all my underwear but Amina found it all and washed it and brought it back. I could not eat or drink anything made in the house, but got Willie to bring me chocolate and *panini* from the bar, the same thing always, twice a day, and beer in cans which I washed in soap till everything tasted of soap and I sicked it all up.

I felt dirty all the time. I washed my hair in the morning, and then again at night, and sometimes in the middle of the day. I bit my fingernails till there was nothing left to hide any dirt and washed my hands so often they become red and sore. I used to go around the house, counting things: silver, pictures, wastepaper baskets, counting out loud, and when I had finished, I counted something else. I went all through the library with the catalogue, every single book in it. I locked up each room I left and then couldn't find the keys and Giuseppe had to come and pick the locks.

I was going mad, Davy. I felt like a house where a brick is missing from a corner and the whole thing is cock-eyed and will fall down. Nothing was as before. Everything was twisted out of line. I stayed in bed in the morning, because of the pills and because I could not go and wake you. I used to wake with a terrible sense of missing something and think how long it would be before I could take another pill. The thought of putting my stockings and shoes on was loathsome so that I had to count down from ten to make myself do it.

I behaved oddly to people and they to me, either being too hearty or just passing by without speaking. Your father slept in his dressing room and I heard him at night, speaking into his tape recorder, but if I went in, he used to look at me with his eyes hooded and take me back to my room and I would lie waiting for the pills to work and hearing the fireworks in Bocca d'Oro.

In the day, I read to your father from *Il Sole* and thought, I really am going mad, reading share prices with the whole world falling down and he used to get cross, saying what a bad reader I was and did I want to starve as well as lose my son? He went out, at strange times of day and night, and would not say where he had been, even when I pleaded with him, and begged him to say whether there had been a message.

I became suspicious. There was so much suspicion. Olgiata really enjoyed himself recording our telephone conversations at the exchange, even when I talked to Oriana in New York, or so he said, and I believed him because he put a young policeman to watch the house from under the pines, until Amina got him one day to come into the kitchen for coffee and *vinsanto* and then he was forced to watch from outside the gate.

Willie kept looking at me, as if about to ask something, as if I knew something important which could tell us where you

121

were or who had taken you. I said to your father that perhaps Willie should go, as he had spoken to the police, and he wasn't going to have much of a Christmas and obviously Oriana really liked him, but he said: No, everybody stays, everybody who was in the house on 15 December stays until Davy is found.

I tried to be cheerful. I was so cheerful, Davy. I said there was no point moping and Willie had come for Christmas and would stay for Christmas. And if Amina started murmuring about the poor little boy with the *camorristi*, the tears running down her big, stupid face, I bit her head off and told her to get on with her work so that she flew round the kitchen till my back was turned.

I could not go to the church, because that fiendish man had sacked Giovanni and taken out a civil action against us for using the cemetery for his mother. Davy, I could have died for nobody to talk to or trust, but for old Herr Hoffmann, who arrived, as I knew he would, the evening that you went away though he looked terribly old and his diabetes was much worse. But when I put my arms round him, and felt his oldness, I was sure we had a chance, even a small one.

He used to go out every day in the morning to the village, taking Willie with him, and they had a good lunch at Nella's. But I knew, all the time, that that ugly head of his was thinking, was never not thinking about where you were and how we could get you back.

He used to come back, about four, with his face red from the cold and the signora's lunch and say, 'What shall we do today? The tower?'

And I ran up the stairs, tripping at the same place as I tripped before, feeling the weight of you, my arms round your armpits and your head lolling to one side.

He said, 'Was the room different from this?'

I'd say, 'I don't know, it was dark, because the lights were off, I didn't see if the drum was here, though you see it, there in the picture, which I was painting that morning.'

He'd say, 'You here, Davy here. William and Giovanni in the attic, fighting the rain. And what was the time?'

'It was quarter past four when I went to bed.'

Or we went to the dining room and he'd walk round it and say, 'What was different then?'

'The stuff on the walls. And the gas fire was on. And the glasses. Two glasses on the fire.'

'Whose glasses were those?'

'One was Giovanni's, for it had the marks he makes on a glass. I don't know who drunk from the second glass.'

'The captain has found the Signora Amina's fingerprints on both glasses.'

'That may be because she washed them up, if that's the word.'

He'd say, '*Naja*, we know that Signora Amina says she washed everything up. So Giovanni came down afterwards and had a glass. And somebody else. Old Giovanni and somebody else. His sister. Or somebody else?'

We always stopped then, because we couldn't get any further.

The weather got better. The wind shifted and there were several cold, blue days. One day, I found Giuseppe climbing the tower and Jakob timing him from below with a stopwatch. Jakob and I went down together to the Faro and timed the walk with the watch but he became so breathless that I did not think he'd make it back up and Giuseppe met us with his taxi. Willie went back to sitting under his tree by the kitchen and I did some gardening. Two crocuses came up by the back door.

Your father said we should have everybody back for Christmas dinner and invite Captain Olgiata. I asked him not to. I wept and shrieked worse than you having a bath in the old days, but he said that I must trust him, as he knew best. Only not to ask Emilio Braggiotti, because he had business of his own. So I asked Willie to go round inviting everybody and I got out your crib and the Christmas presents, even those I had got for you, and sat on my bed, wrapping them and crying and hating your father because he is so selfish.

Then Herr Hoffmann went away to Zürich and I knew something was happening. I thought: Jakob knows something. I felt almost happy that day, I think it was 21 December, as I set up the crib with Willie and made a stable for the Virgin and Child.

Willie was so good at things like that. He threw himself into it, just like with his flower specimens before. But I could see he wanted to say something, even while we were sitting there, and laughing and I watched him roll his courage up into a ball and lower his head and say, not looking at me:

'Why don't you leave him? I'll look after you.'

I didn't understand at first what he meant. I thought he was speaking of you and had gone batty. Then I realised that he meant your father, and I cried, because I was fond of Willie and it was too late. He went on, in a hurry, the words jumping out one after the other, while he stared at one of the figures. I remember it was a wise man, Melchior.

A lot of what he said was true. What had happened was bound to happen in the sort of life we led, cut off from the world, with only rules we had made ourselves; that I was a drudge to your father just I had been to my father. I tried to shut him up, but he hurried on, saying terrible things that I could not bear to hear: that your father staged the burglary for the insurance, that he wasn't fit to be near you. And he said he could find you, because he loved you as much as anybody, and then we would leave the villa and go away, the three of us, to New York or the Bosphorus or anywhere out of this hell.

I felt so sad for him, because it was too late. He did not understand that human beings are not passengers. You cannot just walk off one train and onto another going in the opposite direction. You have to go back to where you started from, back to all the decisions and choices you made and reverse them. Then you can start again.

You see, Davy, he did not realise that it made no difference that I married John Chadwick instead of William Nelson. It did not matter as long as I stayed with one and he stayed with me. Human beings can adapt to anything so long as there is no escape.

Only Jakob knew that, because he had been in hell and

had lost all his family and all his people. But he had learned in that time how to lie and to cheat and to bribe and to do all the things that the people who made the camp thought he was already. Jakob was not like his father, the famous rabbi, who thought that they could survive if they worked hard and made themselves useful. He knew they were in a sort of waiting room. He said he could only buy or steal some time in it. And when he walked out through the camp gates, with the Russians just a few miles away, he said he carried the camp with him and would go on carrying it till the weight became too much for him. God bless him, whichever God it is, because he stole some time for you and me.

I've made myself cry now, thinking about Jakob and Willie. I used to cry all the time then, about the stupidest things, like Christmas presents, until your father said I should go to the Carmelite sisters again to rest. I think he only did not pack me off there and then because of his Christmas dinner and guests.

Even then we didn't get on. In the beginning, we talked about the world outside, because he was interested in foreign affairs and would get excited about America or the Pope but by the time you were born, he read the *Financial Times* and then just *Il Sole* because it was cheaper. I tried to learn about p/es and bond yields, which go down instead of up, but the books he gave me were so complicated and there was so much maths that I never got anywhere.

He was only interested in me as a bit of himself, as his wife. You were his child. The villa was his house. He didn't think of us as separate people, with our own wishes and habits. For years, he and I communicated through you, rather like his mother and all those bonkers women in Bournemouth who talk to people through their dogs: We don't really like her, do we, Spot and that sort of thing. You were a bridge which we could walk over and meet in the middle before going back to what we were doing on our own. Without you, there was only the routine of the house, of buying the newspapers and bossing Amina and drinking a *ramazotti* in the bar and reading the share prices.

He was bored and he blamed me for it, though it wasn't my fault that he wasn't working in the City. He could have taught English or worked in Naples or had a shop like Franco. I couldn't bear to think what would happen if I did go away to the sisters. I prayed for Jakob to come back from Zürich.

FOURTEEN

by Dawn Chadwick

I got my way in one thing, although it took days. I had good tactics. I fought tooth and nail to have our dinner at Signora Nella's, knowing I hadn't got a chance. When I finally gave in, your father had to agree that we not use the dining room. I never wanted to eat in that room again. Even then, your father almost changed his mind, till I had Amina help me lay the table in the tiled hall upstairs and we unlocked the front door.

I thought I would never get through Christmas day. It rained, as it always seemed to at that time. When the clock showed six o'clock, it was all that I could do to get dressed. Amina shrieked when I came into the kitchen and pulled out a horrid comb and brushed my hair for me. As I sat in the chair, with her pulling at the roots and scolding, I wanted just to lie down and fall asleep. I felt as I used to do at the dentist's with the gas in my mouth.

The Olgiatas arrived punctually. I had not met her, but I took against her at once. While he lounged, out of uniform, in the only comfortable chair, she wandered round the library, gaping at things and throwing out stupid remarks. She spent as long before one of my pictures as in front of the Guido and when she came to one of the busts, she passed her hand over the face, and said over her shoulder:

'I like sculpture. I like painting, too, signora, but sculpture is more plastic, don't you think?'

She went over to the bookcases and ran her index finger beneath titles she probably could not read, murmuring, 'Ah, the books, the books.' I thought Willie would burst out laughing.

I know this sounds snobbish, but I did not want them in

127

my house, he lounging and sipping his whisky and computing our wealth and the tax we should pay and she treating the place as if it were hers. She was a copy cat. When the Crespis arrived, she took to dropping names at Oriana and flattening her rs like Franco, till Willie spilled his drink and had to go out for a moment.

Fortunately, Oriana arrived early. She looked so sexy that I could only stare. She stood at the top of the steps, in a black mackintosh and hat, laughing from her scamper in the rain, while her father fumbled with a broken umbrella and a plastic bag. Underneath, she had on just a simple black dress, made of wool, but it hung so well over her small bosoms and waist, that it looked as if it had been made for her and I felt such a slattern and Signora Olgiata looked sick. As she moved to greet the Olgiatas who did not even stand, I heard the rustle of her clothes and felt again as I did at school and was so proud to be her friend.

And she smelt as I imagine Aphrodite smells. Her scent was all over the room. It was like lilies and gin and woodsmoke and racehorses, like the smell of the old house at Bury, all glamour and escape. It was a new scent, which a man had made for her in Paris and it was to be called 'Marchesina' and sold everywhere, even New York. Her father was muttering coarse comments to Olgiata about cats, but I just bathed in the scent, thinking how beautiful and how lucky she would always be.

Only Willie seemed uncomfortable. He kept getting up, to bring the Antinori champagne or more whisky, and when she addressed him, he said only yes or no and went back to talking to Signora Olgiata.

I know Oriana better than any woman and she gets what she wants. She bit her lip and stood up. Signora Olgiata was back on the pictures, leaning on Willie as they stood in front of the Guido and he was pretending to suppress a giggle because his shoulders were shaking from behind. Oriana swished past me, with her train of scent, stood beside them and then touched him on the shoulder with her little finger. I thought a door had banged or a pane broken. The room seemed to shiver as if the rain and the wind had blown through. Willie straightened. And I felt so sad as one always does when two people you love turn in on themselves and their path begins to go away across the field. And I felt happy too because a bit of the past had fallen away and it would be easier now.

Even Franco, not the most observant of men, saw something was up. He buried himself in the books, calling out to Olgiata about the divine Sir Walter, whom the captain probably hadn't heard of. Then he pounced on a book, a Loeb from its red binding, and turned to me and another piece fell away.

'Aha, Dawn. What are the *Annals* doing among the Romantics? The system is breaking down, prose among verse, Latin with Italian. That should be PB Lat, should it not?'

'Oh dear, thank you, Franco, could you put it on the table? It's so silly, Captain Olgiata, but if a book is put back in the wrong place it can take years to find. Willie!' I said looking over at him sternly. He stood so transfixed with Oriana beside him that I burst out laughing and had mercy on him. 'You're jolly lucky I'm not going to tell John, just this once.'

'I suppose you will be leaving the library to the Commune,' said Olgiata. I could have killed him.

Franco came to the rescue. 'What on earth for, Captain? Who would read the books then? But it is worse than I thought, Dawn. Somebody has written in it.' He lifted up the book for all to see that a passage had been marked with two lines in the margin. 'There is an anarchist within.'

'Willie!'

He was looking at the floor and my pretend angry glance went right over his head. I felt something was wrong. So did Oriana. She put her arm through his. Once again I felt the stab of their touch. 'Don't be such a bully, Dawn. Who cares about boring old Tacitus?'

'I do,' said Franco, 'and so should you. Oriana. And you, too, Captain Olgiata, for this passage describes disturbed times such as our own. I shall read it for you, and then construe it into Italian, and English as I used to do at Stonyhurst.'

He began. I could not follow it at first. The sentences were so short and Franco stopped after each one, seeming to wait ever longer between them till I could not bear it, for it was familiar. Franco read as if it had been Italian, his voice coming out of his chest, till the Latin seemed to fill the room, all sharp and heavy. I knew then that it was Willie's favourite passage, which he had read out loud after the hijack, and recited out on the cliff in the Tiberio, because it was about war and violence. And I knew that he had remembered all that I wanted to forget.

I will give it to you in English, Davy, not as Franco did but from the translation, though it's worth knowing Latin just for this bit alone and I wished you had done it as Franco wanted you to but your father said Latin was useless and he had never missed it:

I am entering a work rich in disasters, savage wars, civil strife; even its peace was cruel. Four emperors perished by the sword. There were three civil wars; more wars abroad; often both at once. Things went well in the East, badly in the West. Illyricum was troubled; the Gauls wavered; the full conquest of Britain was achieved and at once abandoned; the Sarmatic and Suevic tribes rose against us; Dacia became famous for catastrophe suffered and inflicted; Parthia, too, nearly drew the sword, duped by a false Nero. Italy itself was stricken by disasters, either wholly new or unknown for centuries. Cities were swallowed up or overwhelmed on the richest part of the Campanian coast. Rome was wasted with fires; her most ancient shrines destroyed; the Capitol itself fired by Roman hands. There were profanations of religious rites, adulteries in high places. The seas were crowded with exiles; and rocky islands stained with murder. Rome itself saw cruelties yet more savage.

Franco put the book down on the table and went back to his seat. Nobody spoke until Signora Olgiata, who was one of those women who cannot stand silence in company, piped up: 'I quite like Latin, but don't you prefer our own Italian, *marchese*? Dante and Moravia and all the classics of literature.'

'I like a bit of everything, Signora. But Mr Nelson, I shall not read the other passage, about Tiberius and his little hobbies down on this coast, splendid as it is, because there are ladies present.' He smiled indulgently at his daughter and I thought what fools parents are, that he thought Oriana, of all people, might be shocked by Tiberius's goings on.

'Now, now, enough of that. This isn't Capri.' I felt restless again. 'It's time to have our presents or you'll all starve. I'll get John. And where is that infernal Giuseppe?'

I knocked on the door of your father's dressing room and entered. He had not changed. He was seated at his desk, talking into his microphone. He did not look up. I stood for a while, thinking that fences were going up all round now and that soon we would not speak to each other at all. And I thought, the others won't come, Giuseppe won't come and Amina won't sit down with us, for though they could not bear to refuse me, they could not bear to come and would make some excuse about the rain or their families.

I went back to the library. I saw everybody smiling at me and I looked down at the presents below the crib, and Franco's plastic bag and the Olgiatas' filthy Perugina chocolates. I saw Willie not knowing whether to hand them out and the laundry basket behind, where I had put Davy's presents, and I wanted to lie down and die.

'Come on, Willie,' said Oriana. 'Let's take Davy's presents up to his room or that fierce Captain will make us pay duty on them.' God bless Oriana, I said to myself, as they lifted up the basket between them. The Olgiatas exchanged knowing glances and smirked and I glared at them, the fools.

I got through that bit, Davy, though how I don't know and I don't know what I received or gave. But the dinner was worse, so much worse. The numbers were so short that I sat them all down at my end and all I could see from my place was empty chairs, with your father's empty chair at the top. It was all right when Amina was serving, because she made jokes and flirted with Franco which seemed so absurd as she was so old and fat and he so gentleman, but afterwards

131

nobody would speak. Willie and Oriana seemed unable to talk to each other. He looked uncomfortable and she, if anything, angry. But nobody could talk to them because their complicity made a sort of wall around them. Every so often, Signora Olgiata threw out some silly thing about the Crespi family or the price of fish or veal, but even she was soon shut up. I just stared at your father's empty place and listened to the rain and the sound of thunder, or maybe it was fireworks from the village. The lights flickered until I asked Willie to turn them off at the mains and he brought up one of the big candelabra from downstairs.

It was then that your father came in. He still had not changed. He was wearing a filthy jumper and he carried a torch. I could hear him better than see him, padding round the table, just outside the circle of light, shining his torch around so that it shone in my eyes, and then lighting Willie's face and the Captain's and Oriana's. He sat down, putting down the torch beside him so it shone full in my eyes and I had to turn away. Then he got up, walked down the table, picked up a dish and started gobbling it with a foul sucking noise, upending the dish so pieces of pasta fell out on his jumper and onto the floor. Then he picked up a bottle, opened it, and raised it to his lips so it came pouring down on him and he had to put it down. He came back to his place with the bottle.

'John, for God's sake, what's happening?'

He got up again, walked back down the table and reached out for some of the small fishes. He stuffed them into his mouth and went back to pacing round us, shining his torch in the faces of each one. Signora Olgiata looked like crying from embarrassment. Franco was on the point of rising, his hand on the back of his chair. Oriana kept turning to Willie, and then to me, for explanation. Willie had a little smile on his face. Only Olgiata looked at ease, following your father with his clever eyes.

'Doctor Chadwick. What are you doing?' Signora Olgiata was trying to be spritely but she reached out to her husband for support.

'Shut up, you bitch.' Your father's voice came out of darkness. 'You are only here so your husband can be my witness.'

'But, Enzo....'

'Be quiet,' said Olgiata.

Your father spoke from the darkness. 'Which of you killed my son?'

I must have screamed because he shone the light at me and then on the others.

'Stop this at once, John.' Franco had spoken.

The torch moved round to Franco. 'I wouldn't pay you the compliment of including you in my suspicion.' He pretended to laugh but went on too long and stopped. 'You are incompetent, even with the help of your slut of a daughter, who treats my house like a brothel. But she's mistaken her man and will have to find another, won't she? Ah she's weeping now, though she hasn't lost a son.'

Willie pushed Oriana out of the torch beam and let it rest on himself. He stared up at your father with cheek written all over his face. 'Go on, old boy,' he said. 'Perhaps Captain Olgiata should be taking notes.'

'Indeed, he should. For it's you that I'm interested in, you at the head of the Christmas table: William Nelson, my oldest friend, and my dear, darling, half-witted Dawn. It was you two who killed my son.'

'Except,' said Willie slowly, 'he isn't your son, old fellow, as you very well know.'

'No, no, no.' It was me talking, screaming, the plates and glasses falling at my feet. 'He's nobody's son. He's Davy.'

I started shivering. My left leg was shaking. It was cold. The door was open, and rain was blowing into the room so that I felt it on my face. The torch shone on the doorway.

Jakob stood on the threshold. He seemed to have grown in size, though perhaps it was his brown coat and his blue hat, both dark from the rain, which made him seem so. Behind him was Giuseppe, almost invisible behind packages and my first thought, Davy, was: Oh no, not presents, please God, not more presents. Giuseppe's arms were covered in dirt up

133

to the elbow and Hoffmann's boots were muddy. Giuseppe tottered to the table and put the packages on the empty chair beside Olgiata. There were two of them, wrapped thickly in oilskin, which was also muddy. One was square and thin and the other big and round, or rather a hemisphere.

Hoffmann wiped his feet and walked towards Olgiata. 'I am sorry we are late,' he said. Then he came down the table and stood beside me. He bent and spoke very quietly in my ear: 'Come, my darling. It is late and we must pick up Davy.'

FIFTEEN

by Dawn Chadwick

The wind was like a wall. Jakob slipped on the steps and we
had to support him. I had no coat and I was wet through
before we reached the car. Giuseppe drove off quickly down
the drive. I looked back out of the car and Olgiata was
standing in the french window lit by the torchlight inside.
He seemed to be trying the door but Giuseppe had
locked it.

Jakob was bent double in the back. His huge wet coat
almost filled the seat. Its skirt was filthy with mud. His eyes
were closed and he was wheezing badly. I snuggled up close
to him and put my arm across his chest, which rose and fell
with his difficult breathing.

'Oh Jakob, you're such a goose. You shouldn't have done
this. Where is he?'

His eyes were still closed. Giuseppe had reached the main
road, and turned full round to look at me.

'Where to, *sorella*?'

'Where to, Jakob?' I hugged him gently.

Giuseppe turned the engine off and then the lights. It was
quite dark. I could hear nothing but the rain and the sound
of Jakob's breathing against my head.

'Jakob, please tell me. Where is he?'

Giuseppe turned the dashboard light on. He turned to me
again. 'Where shall I drive, Dawn?'

I was beside myself. 'For God's sake, please, Jakob, where
is Davy?'

He spoke very softly without raising his head from the
seat-back. 'I don't know.'

'But Jakob, you must know, you found the things. Was
Davy with them?'

'I don't know. You know.'

'Left or right, sister?'

'Oh Giuseppe. Go right, no, left, left.'

Giuseppe started the car and turned left, driving very slowly. He did not turn on the lights. When Jakob began to speak, he stopped again.

'You cannot fool a Swiss banker, Dawn. In the end. It might have worked if the good Doctor Braggiotti had not been arrested. Without him, there was no success in Zürich.'

'What do you mean? Jakob, I don't understand you.'

He coughed, made as if to reach for a pocket, then gave up and spoke again. 'They wanted me to think that Giuseppe had got in, through the tower, because he is thin. Or that the *marchesa* and William Nelson left the door open for special. They did not tell me about Signor Giovanni, catching rain-water in the tower. You told me that. Only you, my darling, tried to tell the truth about Giovanni and I ignored it, because everybody ignores the simple people, the weak and the poor and the mad.'

'Giovanni, you mean it was Giovanni. He wouldn't ever do that. He loves Davy, you know that.'

He was quiet so long I thought he had not heard me over the rain. 'Who made Giovanni do it, Jakob? Tell me. Tell me.'

He spoke at last. 'There was a second glass.'

'John. Willie. John. Oh Jakob, who was it?'

He said nothing, Giuseppe turned on the inside light and looked at me.

'John? How could he do it? To his own son, to his only son. And to his own house, that in the dining room. He's insane.'

He hugged me to his wet, cold chest. It felt different, not strong, but brittle and disturbed. 'Ah, but he is sane. It is poor Giovanni who is mad. Mr Chadwick thought carefully and he thought there was no risk. The pieces were in the old lady's grave, the boy in her closed house, and Signor Giovanni to look after both. You see, he thought there was no risk. He didn't know you are brother and sister. He thought Giuseppe was stupid and didn't know anything and went to Switzerland alone. But Giuseppe is my friend.'

'But where is Davy now? Where is Giovanni? We must find them, Jakob.'

'I don't know. You know.'

'But John knows. For pity's sake, why didn't you ask him?'

'He doesn't know. You know.'

Giuseppe put the car back into gear, but I felt he was still looking at me in the dark. We passed the new villas. I thought: how could I know, if Jakob does not know, if Giuseppe does not know. I could see light from curtained windows coming out into the rain. In front, the lighthouse flashed on and off, on and off.

'Stop!'

We stopped. Giuseppe switched on the inside light, turned round and looked at me again.

'We must get out here. You stay, Jakob, or you'll catch your death. Giuseppe and I will go. To the Tiberio.'

Jakob sighed. The sigh was long and shallow. 'We tried up there already. Mr Nelson took us.'

'Did he take you to the cistern?'

Giuseppe smacked the steering wheel. Jakob sighed again: 'Ah, we knew of no cistern. He did not tell us about the cistern. Maybe only Mr Nelson knew about the cistern, or you and he. You did not tell me everything, my darling.' He shivered. '*Naja*, what do we need for your cistern?'

'I have a rope,' said Giuseppe. 'It is not easy.'

I got out of the car. The rain went straight through my dress again and I began to shiver. Giuseppe brought me a coat and then started helping Jakob out of the car.

'No, no. You must stay. We won't be long. Giuseppe, let's take him in to, oh I don't know, do you know the people here?'

'I am coming. Young Giuseppe will give my injection.'

From his pocket he took out something that looked like a fountain pen, handed it to Giuseppe and slipped his arm out of his coat. Giuseppe steadied him and jabbed it right through his shirt into the arm.

We set off through the houses, Giuseppe leading with a

137

torch. The rain sliced down the hillside into our faces. We had not reached the terraces before Jakob halted and sat down.

'Giuseppe, it is hopeless. We must take him back.' I had to shriek above the wind.

'No, Dawn. This is my business. Signor Giuseppe, please help me.'

Giuseppe put the coil of rope round my neck and handed me the torch. I shone it on the old man. Giuseppe squatted down and lifted him onto his back. He swayed in the wind, then found his footing, grinned and took the torch back.

Jakob gestured at me. I came close so I could feel his breath.

'Why did he take Davy from the old lady's house?'

'Because he thought Davy was his.'

'Did you tell him that?'

'I had to, Jakob. He knew it wasn't John.'

I felt his sigh on my cheek. Oh Jakob, oh Davy, you must understand. Please, Davy, you must understand. I was talking to you, going up that hill, tripping on the terraces and catching at Jakob's coat as they plunged ahead of me. I was shouting your name but nobody was hearing me. I wanted you to understand. I knew no men. I only knew my father. And I felt so sorry for him, at the end of his life, all alone and drifting away. I wanted him to love me again. Oh Davy, I never knew it would cause all this evil.

As we got near the top of the cliff, Giuseppe began to run, I called at him to wait for me, but he did not hear, and I just saw the torch beam swinging up and down ahead of me. It turned a corner and I tasted salt in the rain on my lips. I called again. I thought they would leave me up on the hill and I ran till my heart was bursting and till I saw the light again.

They were at the entrance to the garden. The iron gate had been wrenched open. Jakob was slumped on the step. Giuseppe was chafing his ankles.

'I would like to stop here. Go on, with Signor Giuseppe.'

I followed Giuseppe round, holding his coat and feeling

the edge of the wall with the other hand. At the cliff edge, he fastened one end of the rope to the wall and the other round his waist. He gave me the torch.

I could not see at first. The rain was in my eyes and I had to wipe them. I shone the torch along the cliff edge. The path had fallen away in lots of places, but halfway along the wall on the cliff side, there was a ledge and what looked like a hole in the wall. I remembered it. To show off, Willie had run along the path and slipped and only held his footing by gripping the roots on the path. He had wanted to show he was a daredevil, that he could take risks, now that there weren't any except those he made himself and his friend was dead on the runway.

'Keep the torch there, sister. Please do not move it.'

Giuseppe disappeared. I dared not move the torch off the ledge, but I could not even hear him over the rain and the wind. I strained my ears to hear something. I shouted after him. Then suddenly he was there, first a hand, and then his whole body, all thin and agile, crouching on the ledge and holding on to something in the wall.

'Bravo, Giuseppe, bravo.' I found I was jumping up and down.

He could not hear me. He extended his arm and beckoned me, just as Willie had done.

'I can't, Giuseppe, please, no. I can't. Please, please, no. It was day then and the sun shining and the path was all right then.'

He beckoned me again.

'No, I can't, I can't.'

'Try.'

I turned round. Jakob was beside me, his face pressed against the wall, wheezing in great big gulps. 'You see, I cannot, and only you know how to get in. You have the rope. Courage, my darling.'

He took the torch and shone it on the ledge. I gripped the wet rope and stepped out. My foot slipped and all my weight came on my arms. I found my footing, took a step and then slipped again. I could hear the sea below me, breaking on the rocks, with a steady beat, like a drum. Oh Davy, I prayed. I prayed that you were safe, even if I fell. And that if I fell, it was the price of your being safe and not of my doing wrong. And I prayed that God should not let what Jakob had done, and what Giuseppe had done, come to nothing and that if I fell, they should find you, well. And I prayed for my father and I prayed for you, Davy, that if I fell, all would be well.

'Bravo, sister.' Giuseppe had me in his arms. My head was spinning. It felt as if it were falling, down to the rocks below. I pushed my stomach against the iron gate and stayed there, till I had finished being sick.

'How did you open it before?'

I felt down the wall till I came to the hole, where Willie had found the key. The metal was cold, much colder than the wall. 'Follow me, Giuseppe. It's quite difficult.'

Inside, it was dry. The place smelt of dust and rot and a sweet herb, French lavender probably. There were steps down. I heard the drip of rain, where the cistern was open to the sky, but could see nothing. A bat squealed and Giuseppe jumped. I could still hear the drumming of the sea below.

I shone the torch on the floor. Amid the brambles. I could see pieces of blue pavement. Willie had broken off a bit and put it in Polunin and said: This will be my souvenir of you if my memory really goes. Poor, mad Willie.

'To the left, Giuseppe, quietly,' I said. He hesitated, but followed me.

The brambles were waist-high. We stepped into a pool of water that covered my shoes. The drumming was louder now, a slow regular beat. I followed the sound of the drum. Giuseppe began to lag. He was shivering and muttering under his breath.

'Stay here. It will be all right.'

A bramble tore my face. Another pulled at my legs. One wrapped round my waist and I had to break it with my hands till they were bleeding. I pulled off my coat and put it over my head. I pushed forward. Something tore my hair but I pushed forward, towards the sound of the drum. I turned my back and leaned with all my might, till something broke and

140

I fell on my bottom.

I fell into dust and old droppings. There was a red light flickering on the brick vault. I stood up. In the light of the fire, Giovanni was squatting on his haunches, a half-empty brandy bottle by his side. Round his neck was your drum and he had a drumstick in each hand. He stopped playing and looked at me, his head on one side.

On the ground at his feet was a red mackintosh, which rose and fell, as if there was something small and alive within it. Then your head came out, your hair tangled and your face filthy and full of sleep and you looked at me, and our eyes crossed and will never uncross again.

SIXTEEN

by Dawn Chadwick

We did not go home. Giovanni was bleeding a lot, from where Giuseppe cut his face with the bottle till you stopped him, and Jakob could not speak any more. We found him sitting on the ground, and I showed you to him, and Giovanni carried him down on his back, though he was bleeding badly and I was all cut on the face, too, from the brambles.

We drove straight to the Carmelites and Dr Carrai came out in his pyjamas and put Jakob straight to bed with Giuseppe in the same room. Then he sewed up poor Giovanni's face and the sister gave you a bath and let me sleep in the same bed as you.

I kept falling into sleep, but each time I woke myself so I could feel you, small and warm and still smelling of woodsmoke, fitting so neatly in my lap. When I woke up, the sun was shining and you had your arms round my neck and I thought: Just this moment, for ever and ever and ever.

Jakob was a little better when we went in to him. His white hair was spread across the pillow and his face had turned waxy, but he could speak. He wanted to kiss you, but you were shy of him and of me, and you stood by the door on one leg. Olgiata came, looking so small and out of place in his uniform, and Jakob whispered something to Giuseppe and Giuseppe took the Captain outside and that was the end of it and I don't know what happened and I don't care.

I wouldn't let your father come, but then Giuseppe said it was time and went off to get the *notaio*. I took you out into the courtyard, and you tried to catch the goldfish in the pond in the middle, and when your father came, you were very shy and hid behind me. Afterwards, the fussy little man came down with the papers for me to sign and I put my signature just by your father's, signing away the house and everything in it to Jakob and his heirs, and then the document for the annuity which was fifty million a year and far more than we needed or deserved. Then the man came from the Banca Commerciale, which was Braggiotti's main creditor and was winding up his affairs, and Jakob must have satisfied him on what we owed because we never heard any more from him.

I did not question you at all, Davy, and when you asked: Why did you go away, I just said I was sorry and kissed you and I think you forgave me but I couldn't tell and never will. At night I cried a lot, about you and about Jakob, and it sometimes woke you up and you told me not to cry and put your arms round my neck and I was so happy, Davy, that I cried even more.

It was after the Banca Commerciale man had gone that Giuseppe said that Jakob wanted to go home. Dr Carrai wouldn't let him but Giuseppe just started packing his things and paid his bill and our bill. We hired a minibus and Giovanni carried the old man down to his wheelchair. He was still wearing his blue hat.

He was too weak to fly from Naples. Giuseppe was going with him on the train. They took a whole carriage to themselves. You ran up and down the platform but I could not look and I sat, on a tub of oleanders, while the guard walked up banging the wheels of the train and Giuseppe ordered everybody about in his best suit. Then the train began to move and I could not look, and I felt it moving, away from the platform, gathering speed under the bridge and past the ruined factories, and when I looked up it had disappeared. And I screamed among the oleanders till the guard took me away.

He died on 25 January of that year.

We got one postcard, that was all. He left you the villa, and everything in it, as Giuseppe said he would, but he made a condition that you go to Zürich and be his son's apprentice when you were sixteen. That is why we are going to send you there, or why you are there, for Jakob always knew best.

It is not that you are paying him back for all we owed,

because he wasn't like that and he never blamed anybody, except perhaps Braggiotti who should have known better and has gone to America now. You see Braggiotti needed the money as badly as your father, because they had really only borrowed all those shares and had to pay cash for them once the stock market started falling, and so he helped fake all those messages from the kidnappers for the insurance, or so Giuseppe said but I'm not sure I've got it quite right.

We could not pay Jakob back in generations. He always thought you would be a great craftsman and expert, as he was himself, and perhaps one day Herr Ariel will make you his partner, if you work hard, and it won't be *Kunstauction Hoffmann* but *Hoffmann und Chadwick* which will look so smart. And the *annualità* is far too much for just us two, really just me because your father doesn't go out any more and I just buy *Gente* and beer to drink while I'm ironing, which doesn't cost much and the laundry brings quite a lot, so I save a bit for you.

Because I do not really understand why your father did what he did, or what Willie thought he was doing, I don't blame them either. I know your father is not capable of considering anybody else and perhaps he wanted to hurt me, for being his wife and living with him so long, and he may have thought it didn't matter so much once he suspected you weren't really his son. I never knew how much he hated the villa until I saw what he made Giovanni do in the dining room.

And perhaps Willie really thought he could bribe me to run off with him once he found out that John had taken you. Poor Giovanni did not know he was doing wrong, when one person told him to take you to his mother's and another to take you to the Tiberio. Perhaps they didn't know they were doing wrong either. Perhaps the exercise books and the tapes will tell you, perhaps not.

I thought of leaving your father and living just with you because I haven't had much luck with men. But then I didn't know where to go and there was no point being in Ascona with Jakob gone and, anyway, I've done enough damage and they say that boys should have a man in the house, though I can't see why. We do not talk very much, and the awful Pasquale reads to him and keeps trying to cadge things, but the house is big and we don't get under each other's feet, especially with all the laundry to do. Giuseppe helps a lot with the house, thought he has become terribly bossy and talks about Jakob all the time, which infuriates me.

Willie came back once, that summer, unexpectedly. I was in the kitchen, ironing, and he sat down at the table, with his head in his hands. I knew he was going to say something, and I knew he was beginning to understand and I kept pretending that the iron wasn't working and made you come down to play in the kitchen which made you cross and then went up myself to keep an eye on Pasquale.

And at the back door, when he turned back as if to tell me what he wanted to tell me, I interrupted and said perhaps he would not be coming to the villa so much, now he was in Capri.

I can see you through the bars, playing with old Bot. You are so small to carry such a burden.